Easy Kill

Charles M. DuPuy

Easy Kill

An EZ Kelly Novel

Charles M. DuPuy

Written Dreams Publishing

Green Bay, WI 54311

Editor: Brittiany Koren
Cover Art Designer: Barbra Sprangers
Interior Layout Designer: Amanda Dix

Category: Mystery/Suspense
Description: *Will travel agent hopeful, EZ Kelly, be able to take the terror cell down before she gets herself killed?*
Hard Cover ISBN: 978-1-7320511-0-2
Paperback ISBN: 978-1-7320511-1-9
Ebook ISBN: 978-1-7320511-2-6
LOCN: Catalog info applied for.
First Edition published by Written Dreams Publishing in February, 2018.

Green Bay, WI 54311

In memory of the Big Guy: CFL

Prologue

"**R**PG!"

I caught the flash in my night vision goggles at the same instant my team leader, Captain Baqua, shouted the warning. The rocket-propelled grenade raced at us from our left flank, my side of our formation, out of a cluster of boulders.

I hit the deck.

It exploded beyond us, striking a rocky promontory and raining debris over us.

Unhurt, I turned towards its origin and spotted six—no nine—no, more like a dozen Taliban fighters racing at us, their AK-47s spraying our position as they closed the distance.

Being a woman has its advantages. I'm designated as a non-combat soldier, a CST, or Cultural Support Team member. I'm along for the ride, trained to interact with the women in the villages we enter. The US Army taught me how to speak Arabic, and the village women often give up information to me, woman to woman, that help us find the bad guys.

The army also made sure I knew how to use a rifle, a knife, and my body to defend myself. My father taught me everything he knew, too. He's a retired captain in the US Army Special Forces. After he and Mom went and named me EZ, he figured he'd better teach me how to kick butt.

My birth certificate says my name is Esther Zane Kelly, but that's not how things worked out. Esther is my dad's mother's first name, and Zane is Mom's mother's maiden name. Both of my grandmas got recognition by my born-to-please parents. For a short time, I was Esther, until the day when Grandma Esther got pissed when she couldn't tell which Esther my parents were talking to. Okay, so Esther got dumped and my parents considered Zane, but Dad rejected it. He didn't want people calling me Zany. Always short and on point, Dad suggested they shorten it to EZ. It quickly took hold. It wasn't until I got older and started growing boob buds that the potential for misunderstanding and lame jokes reared its ugly head. By then, Dad had taught me everything he knew about self-defense, and I feared no one.

I hugged the ground, watching the Taliban fighters charge our position as M4 rifle fire answered their AK-47 chatter. When lead started whapping the ground around me, I went on the offensive.

Flipping off my safety, I fired three-round bursts at the shadowy figures running at me. That gave me ten groups of three from my 30-round magazine. I didn't count but saw the effects of my fire.

When my slide stayed back, magazine depleted, I reached for a replacement, but I'd run out of time. A Taliban fighter was racing toward me, his AK-47 empty. He held it by the barrel like a club, intent upon separating my head from my body with a roundhouse swing.

I dropped my M4 and stood in his path. At the same time, I drew my Ka-bar knife, held it at my side, and waited.

The Taliban fighter planted his feet and began his swing at my head.

My cue.

When he'd committed to his swing, I sank to my knees, allowing his AK-47 to pass harmlessly over my head. I stepped into him, planting my Ka-bar in the left side of his chest, blade held parallel, not vertical, so it slid between his ribs. As I felt it slide home, I twitched the blade left-right-left, allowing the knife's double-cutting edge to rearrange his heart and lungs.

He made a last-ditch effort to bring his rifle around for another swing at me, but he'd run out of time. With a bubbly gasp that stank of rotting teeth, he sagged against my knife hand. His jaw dropped open and an opium pouch fell free. Ground poppy 'courage' at work. I slipped the blade out, allowing him to drop lifeless at my feet.

I scrambled to pick up my M4 and replace the mag, preparing

myself for more attackers. I scanned the area with my night vision goggles, but saw no movement. The firefight had ended.

In the silence that followed, my team leader called for a count. Each of us responded by yelling our names. Except one. Sergeant Pickerel, known to all of us as Fish, didn't answer. He'd taken one in the head. Died instantly.

Captain Baqua moved amongst us, came to my position, and saw what I'd done.

"Jesus, EZ!" he breathed. Then, "Well done."

A man of few words.

As we made our way back to our forward operating base outside Jalalabad, I had time to assess my feelings. I'd never killed another human being before, and sticking a blade into someone is as up-close and personal as it gets. In the end, I decided that a sense of relief best described how I felt. Relief that I got to hike to the base and not get carried back, like my fallen comrade, Fish.

I recalled my dad's words, passed to me during a lull in one of my training sessions with him. "Taking the life of another human being is the worst feeling you can experience." Then he added, "Unless you're doing it to save your own skin."

Once we were at our FOB, we separated to check our gear and wash away the residue of battle. When I emerged from my quarters in a clean Army t-shirt and multicam trousers, my blond ponytail pulled through the back of my cap, the chaplain was there to greet me. I guessed he'd been told what I'd done. I clasped my arms in front, conscious that my t-shirt revealed my braless chest.

"How are you feeling, Sergeant Kelly?" he said, a searching glance of my face in his kind eyes.

"Better than I thought I'd be, to be honest," I replied, making solid eye contact.

"Do you want to talk about it?" he offered.

"There's not a whole lot to talk about, sir. I did what I had to do."

"Sometimes reality takes a while to soak in. Right now, you may be feeling a little numb. If you need to talk about it anytime, I'm here for you."

"Thank you, sir. I'll keep that in mind."

He reached out and grasped my hands with his. "Do you mind if I say a quick prayer, EZ?" he asked.

"I'd like that, sir."

We prayed together, and then went our separate ways.

Afterwards, I never felt the need for more counseling. I'd done what I had to do, done what I was trained to do. If I hadn't, I wouldn't be here. Simple, really. Kill or be killed.

Down time always followed our return to base, and my thoughts turned to Paul. He was part of a Special Forces team in Kandahar, while my team was based in Jalalabad. He might as well have been on the other side of the moon for all we got to see each other.

I thought back to my first encounter with Paul, half way through my junior year. Our school catered to military brats, so it came as no surprise that the principal planned a self-defense contest amongst the students. Participation was voluntary, and classes were suspended for the rest of the day, so all could watch.

I told Dad about it, and he asked if I wanted to join in. Since he'd trained me from my toddler days to be able to defend myself, teaching me what he'd learned as a Special Forces officer, I felt I needed his approval. I said I'd like to try. He cautioned me to remember that some of the moves I knew could hurt someone badly, even kill them.

"But you've got a level head on your shoulders, EZ, and I'm sure you'll do fine."

With his blessing, I signed up.

The contest day arrived. Each class had its participants, boys against boys, girls against girls. Each round's winner could challenge the next class's winner, if they chose to do so. Trophies would go to each class winner, both girls and boys, with a big trophy to the overall winner.

The contest was overseen by the athletic director who had his black belt in Karate, to ensure no serious punches were thrown. Pushing, tumbling, and leg sweeps were fine, but no elbows, fists, knees or feet could strike an opponent.

The athletic director blew his whistle, reviewed the rules, and two freshman girls faced off. Watching their tentative, awkward moves, I wondered if that's what I had looked like two years earlier.

Sophomore entrants came next.

Then it was my class's turn, girls first. There were four of us, so two fought until one won, then I fought my opponent and won. I faced off against the other winner, and took her down. I was the Junior girls' champ!

The junior boys' contest took a little longer, with eight entrants. When the victor was declared, the athletic director asked me if I wanted to challenge the boys' winner. It surprised him when I said yes.

My opponent grinned and bobbed his head in anticipation of taking me down. Then we were on the mat, and the signal to begin was given.

I wasted no time.

Feinting a rush at him, I saw him shift his weight backwards, giving me the opening I hoped for. I rushed him, threw my leg behind him and pushed, using his own momentum to take him down. He impacted the mat with a resounding thump.

A pin dropping could've been heard in the auditorium.

Then a few people clapped, and soon everyone applauded me and my move.

I reached down to help my fallen foe to his feet, but his ego ignored my outstretched hand. Trophy number two: All-Around Junior Champ!

I watched four senior girls fight. I didn't think the winner deserved it. The best one got careless. It reminded me not to take an opponent for granted.

The athletic director asked me if I wanted to challenge the senior girls' winner.

I said I'd pass.

He didn't look surprised.

There were sixteen senior boys entered, so their session took much longer.

The number got down to four.

Then two.

I could tell that one of them was the most accomplished, most confident.

I was right. He won. The audience cheered.

The athletic director held up a hand for silence, then asked the senior girls' winner if she wanted to challenge the winning boy.

She blushed and said no.

"In that case, I declare the competition ended," he announced.

I spoke up. "I'd like to challenge him."

The silence was deafening.

The athletic director stared at me, head cocked. "Are you sure, Miss Kelly?"

"Yes, sir," I said, my voice calm.

"Let's do it, then!" he shouted, and beckoned the two of us onto the mat.

"You both know the rules. Let's have a clean fight, and may the best..." he nearly said 'man', and recovered with "May the best competitor win!"

Turned out, the young man had skills similar to mine. At one point, I wondered if Dad was moonlighting, he was that good. Back and forth we went, feinting, counter-feinting, alert to shifts in balance, an overweighting of one foot over the other.

When we'd exhausted the chance of finding and taking advantage of the obvious, we began throwing blows, which we stopped before contact was made. He used a blocking move against my punches, and I blocked his as well.

It turned into a well-choreographed dance, each move met by the other as we circled the other on the mat. I sensed an opening, and swung a roundhouse punch at my opponent's temple, stopping inches from delivering it.

He hadn't blocked.

A giddy feeling erupted inside me, distracted me, and he directed a similar blow at my temple, which I failed to block.

"Enough!" shouted the athletic director. "I declare you both champions! Both your names will go on the trophy!"

The auditorium erupted with shouts and applause.

I reached my hand out to my opponent. He clasped it in a solid, firm handshake, then leaned in to say, "Hi. I'm Paul Miller. You won."

"I'm EZ Kelly. It was a draw," I replied.

"No. You delivered the first unblocked blow." He smiled warmly.

"I learned a lot today." I returned his smile.

"I learned more," he said. He draped an arm over my shoulder and turned to wave at the cheering crowd.

For the first time in my life the gesture felt comforting, not threatening.

"Want to get something to eat?" he asked.

The competition over, we were free to leave.

"Sure. Sounds good," I said. "I'll go change. Meet you out front in fifteen minutes."

He stood waiting when I stepped outside. I looked him over as I strolled to meet him. I guessed he was around six-two, which felt nice since I'm five-ten. He had broad shoulders and a narrow waist, and he radiated self-confidence standing there. Did I mention blond hair cut short, and piercing blue eyes? Oh, and strong brows set above a narrow nose, thin lips, and a cleft chin. I'd seen all this during our skirmish, but now I could absorb his handsome looks without distraction.

I could sense him doing the same to me, and I hoped he liked what he saw. I never took much stock in my appearance, though I was aware I had an edge on many of my friends.

"Thought you'd gotten cold feet and bolted on me," he said in greeting.

"I considered it, but curiosity won out."

He laughed. "C'mon, let's go to Frankie's."

I knew Frankie's establishment. It was a good three miles from school. "Isn't that a long walk?" I asked.

"It is, but I've got a car."

"Of course you do! Let's go, then."

His car turned out to be a ten-year-old sedan, but it was spotless inside and out. Clearly, he took pride in it.

"This a gift from your parents?"

"Nope. Bought it with money I earned on different jobs."

"Nice." I ran a hand over the dashboard.

Frankie's, at that hour, was quiet, and we grabbed a booth. We ordered sandwiches and water. Lots of water.

Finished eating, I launched into the questions I'd been saving since we'd fought.

"How'd you get so good at self-defense, Paul?"

"Easy. I mean, it was easy. Looks like I'm having trouble with your name. I like it, don't get me wrong. It's… I don't know. Yes, I do. It suits you. It's you!"

"Thanks. That's sweet. I'm sure you can imagine the troubles I've had with it. Learning self-defense has helped. So, answer my question."

He blushed. He actually blushed. "Like I started to say, it was easy. My dad's an Army Ranger, retired now, and he thought I should know how to take care of myself, so he taught me everything he knew."

I could feel a silly grin forming on my lips as he spoke. Noticing, he asked, "What?"

"We share similar backgrounds. Dad was Special Forces and he felt the same way about me. He taught me what he knew, too."

"That explains a lot."

"It does," I said.

"Maybe we could spar together, practice our moves. It'd be a change, maybe give us a different perspective," Paul suggested.

"Why not? I like the idea."

After that, Paul and I met and sparred together on a regular basis. Over time, we developed moves that made us even better.

Dad came to watch our sparring once. After about ten minutes, he nodded his head slowly and said, "You're as good as your old man now, EZ. No, that's not true. You're better."

His words filled me with pride.

As time passed, Paul and I were drawn closer and closer together.

After an exceptionally strenuous workout one day, Paul stepped into me and kissed me with unbridled passion.

I returned his kiss, melting into him. Soon we were horizontal, hauling our clothing out of the way, shivering in the heat of the moment.

In a blur, my reputation as a virgin in the junior class was a distant memory, replaced by far more pleasurable memories. Our first awkward encounter ended in a heartbeat, but our subsequent unions of lovemaking lasted much longer.

As graduation neared, we talked about Paul's plans. He was a bright student, and he knew that a year of college could be a big help to a career military person's success. He'd decided long before he met me to make the military his life, and hoped he'd be good enough to qualify for Special Forces.

My senior year was a painful blur. With Paul's college three states away, we managed to see each other at Thanksgiving and again at Christmas. The spark between us continued, but it seemed less explosive. Or was I imagining things?

Springtime found me immersed in planning my own future. I chose to join the army, too, but never thought of it as a career. Just something to fill my time and gain experience. College would come first.

After Paul finished his year of college, he enlisted in the army. We stayed in touch by email and an occasional Skype call as he moved through training. He was offered training for Special Forces, and I went with his parents to his graduation.

Since then, five years have slipped by.

I got my college degree, and with it, the urge to become a travel agent. First, though, I needed to serve my country and show off what Dad taught me. I'm sure Paul's gone way past my skill level, with all the combat he's seen. I'd still like to spar with him again.

At the end of my second tour, I'd had enough. Thoughts of becoming a travel agent began to make more sense to me than speaking Arabic to Afghani women and children, or firing my M4 into charging Taliban fighters. The Army's gift to me was an enormous self-confidence. I was ready for my life's next chapter, but I didn't know then how much I'd need the skills gained during the time in the US Army.

Chapter One

**Six Months Later—Day One
Miami Beach, Florida**

I looked up as the lobby door of the Adriatic Hotel swung wide and a man strolled towards the reception counter, his eyes everywhere but on me. The lobby was empty. Except for me, the lone desk clerk, he had the place to himself. A glance at the wall clock raised my caution flag. Most guests weren't checking in at two-twenty in the morning, not without luggage, not in Miami Beach. I reasoned that maybe he'd already registered and was returning from a night on the town.

As he approached the front counter, I took in his features. Somewhere around five-eight, five-ten, slight build, dressed casually in jeans and sneakers, wearing a windbreaker, right hand in his side pocket. His hat got my attention. A broad-billed baseball cap was snugged down low over his brow, hiding his eyes and nose from view. His mouth, the only part of his face I could see, stretched taut across the lower part of his face. A man on a mission.

As he shuffled up to the counter in front of me, I smiled and said, "Good evening, sir. May I help you?"

That turned out to be the question that pushed his button.

He yanked his right hand out of his windbreaker pocket. In it, he clutched a compact semi-auto pistol. He brought it to bear directly at my face.

"Step back," he commanded, his voice strong, confident.

I raised my hands and complied, backing away from my side of the counter.

He planted his left hand on the counter and vaulted over, landing smoothly in front of me, his pistol never leaving my face.

"What's your name, honey?" he demanded, his alert eyes sweeping over my blonde ponytail and down the length of my pale blue pantsuit.

"I'm EZ. What's yours?" I replied evenly, my eyes studying his posture, his eyes.

"Funny!" he spat out.

"Funny? I like it. Has a certain ring to it," I said, smiling at him.

"Shut up and open the safe!" he barked.

The safe he referred to sat under the counter, accessible to the hotel staff on duty. It held cash, credit card receipts, and the occasional items left by guests for safekeeping.

"Are you trying to get enough money to buy a real gun?" I asked him, a disarming smile on my face.

It had the desired effect. He glanced down at the gun in his hand, giving me the opening I needed. I stepped into him, my left hand clamping down on the gun, my right driving his head backwards and into the wall behind him.

His head rebounded, leaving a deep imprint, the negative image of the back of his head in the plaster. As he staggered from the blow, I yanked the handgun from his grasp, dropped it on the desk, and spun him around. My left arm circled his neck and I applied steady pressure to his carotid arteries.

"Who's outside waiting for you?" I asked him, my mouth inches from his right ear.

"Fuck you!" he wheezed.

His pupils dilated, and blackness overtook him as I continued to squeeze off the blood flow to his brain.

When he went limp, I lowered him to the floor, then searched his pockets. I found his wallet in a back pocket. Inside was a New Jersey driver's license with a picture and a name. The picture was his. The name: George DeSalva. "Thought you told me your name was 'Funny.' You're a long way from home, George," I whispered to his inert body.

I bound his hands and feet with strong twine the hotel kept on hand to tie parcels, then leaped over the counter, mimicking the move he'd made moments before.

"Time to go meet 'Fuck You,'" I told the sleeping 'Funny' George.

I sauntered to the lobby door and pushed it open, stepping out onto the covered entryway. A car sat idling less than ten feet beyond the door, passenger door open, waiting, no doubt, for 'Funny' George.

I strolled casually over to the driver's side door, noting that the window was down.

"Hey, hi," I called out, keeping my voice calm and casual. "George sent me out to get you. He needs your help."

The driver, taken by surprise, looked my way. "What's he want?" he asked, clearly confused.

"He can't carry everything by himself," I explained.

"Oh. Okay."

He swung his door open and stuck out his left leg, bracing to stand up. He got half way out when I slammed the side of my left hand into his neck. The impact drove him sideways, his head whacking the front door post with a satisfying crunch. Then it rebounded.

He sagged to the pavement, limp, unmoving.

"Guess I don't need to tie you up, Mister Fuck You."

I had a look around for more threats. Seeing none, I hurried back inside to call 9-1-1.

A police cruiser carrying two officers screeched up to the hotel entrance within minutes, lights and siren leading the way. They emerged from the cruiser with their hands resting on their sidearms, ready and wary.

I met them at the door, smiling, wearing my calm face, doing my best to de-escalate their level of alertness. After giving them a speedy summary of what had happened, I pointed out the unconscious driver.

"That's one," I said. "The other one's inside, behind the counter."

One of the officers approached the unconscious driver while the second one followed me inside to the reception counter. He moved with caution, his steps deliberate, edgy. A big man who was over six feet tall, his dark brown hair in a crew cut, he swept the area with piercing grey eyes. I guessed his age in the low thirties.

"We can use the door. It's easier than climbing over." I gestured at the door to the left of the counter that led to the reservations desk. I punched the four-digit code into the keypad, then swung the door open. I stepped through first and pointed down.

"There's the other one. I put his gun on the desk there," I said with a sweep of my hand.

The officer followed my direction, saw the man bound on the floor, his bleary eyes staring back at us. Seeing the officer, resignation dominated his expression.

The officer reached for the mic clipped to his shoulder strap, keyed it, requested a second cruiser. "We've got two suspects," he told dispatch. Then he faced me.

"I'm Officer Jackson, Miss. Tell me what happened here." He took a small notebook and pen from his breast pocket as he spoke.

I summarized what had taken place. Finished, I said, "Guess that's it."

Officer Jackson stared at me a moment, assessing me. "Who else helped you?" he asked, his eyes searching the lobby.

"It was just me, Officer. As you can see, there's nobody else around." My arm swept the empty lobby as I spoke.

"What's your name?" he asked, realizing he hadn't secured that detail at the onset.

"E Z Kelly, sir."

Officer Jackson looked up from his notebook. "What's that? A nickname?"

"No, sir. It's the name I ended up with after my parents named me Esther Zane Kelly. To avoid offending my grandmas, they shortened it to EZ. You can guess how EZ became easy, right? They considered naming me Earwyna which means *friend of the sea*, but in the end, they thought better of it. Here, I'll get my ID." I reached into a cubby hole for my purse.

As I did so, Jackson's left hand clamped down on my purse and he wrenched it from my grasp. I had a brief opening when I could've driven my right elbow into his solar plexus, disabling him. I chose not to.

He backed away from me, which was a professional move on his part, and opened my purse. I watched him reach inside and feel around, I assumed for a weapon. Finding none, he held the purse out to me.

I took it, found my wallet and pulled out my driver's license for him.

He took it from me, glanced at it long enough to confirm my name, then returned it. "So, how's that name working out for you?" he asked, a faint smile flirting with his stern mouth.

"It gets better every day, sir," I replied as I swept a wisp of hair behind my right ear.

"I'm guessing your self-defense skills may have something to do with that."

"You could be right," I allowed.

"We'll need you to come to the station, give us your full statement so we can process these guys." It was more of a command than a request.

"My relief comes on at seven. I'll be there soon after, okay?"

Officer Jackson glanced at the clock. "Three hours. Yeah, that's fine. It'll take us awhile to process these birds. I'll make sure it takes at least that long."

It surprised me that nearly two hours had slipped by since the man strolled through the lobby door and turned a dull night into an adventure. *Time flies when you're having fun,* I thought.

At that moment the lobby door opened, and two more officers strode in. Backup had arrived.

Officer Jackson briefed them on what had happened.

After curious glances my way, they helped the bound man to his feet and replaced the twine with handcuffs, securing his hands behind his back. One of the officers searched the man's pockets for ID and weapons, and found his wallet. He bagged it.

At the same time the second officer secured the pistol, noting that it was a subcompact 9mm. He removed the magazine, ejected a round in the chamber. All three items went into another evidence bag.

"You're lucky he didn't pull the trigger, Miss," the officer commented.

Maybe he did. When I'd grabbed George's gun hand, I'd forced the slide back. It opened the chamber just enough to make it impossible to fire, no matter how many times he tried to pull the trigger. Instead I said, "I guess I am," doing my best to sound like I'd dodged a bullet.

They escorted their prisoner out to the second cruiser. Jackson's partner had already handcuffed the driver and moved him into the back of the first cruiser. I appreciated good police work. Separation kept the two men from putting their heads together and agreeing on a common statement while on the way to their interrogation.

As I followed Officer Jackson outside, he told me a tow truck would be along soon to haul off the now-abandoned vehicle. "Evidence," he added. Then he reminded me to come by after my shift ended.

"Don't worry. I'll be there," I reassured him.

They climbed into their cruisers and drove off. The silence that followed me into the empty lobby was deafening.

I returned to the desk chair behind the counter and sat down. I drew in several long breaths, held each briefly, then exhaled slowly.

It worked to calm and relax me, blowing off the residual adrenaline circulating in my bloodstream.

I reviewed what had happened. Something didn't seem right.

The stickup man was clean, well groomed, well dressed, not the sort you'd expect to jam a gun in your face and demand money. And then there was the driver. He didn't look like somebody in need of cash, either. Maybe they were into drugs, needed money for a hit or two. Then again, maybe not.

With nothing to do and time to kill, I found myself reminiscing over my freshman high school days, and one particularly annoying junior student. Lunch was over, and we milled about in the hall, getting books from lockers, preparing for afternoon classes. He spotted me and stepped into my space.

"Hey there, EZ. Just how *easy* are you? Me, I'm easy, and I'm thinking you and I could get together, you know, and do the horizontal mambo."

Two of his buddies stood to the side, guffawing and slapping their thighs, enjoying the show.

"Leave me alone," I said in a firm voice, looking him in the eye.

"Oh, wow. What a turn on! Now you've really got me. What do you say we go for it?"

I stepped into his space and waved my right hand in a wide circle, drawing the attention of the gawkers. At the same time, I drove the straight fingers of my left hand into his solar plexus—as Dad had shown me—then withdrew them in a flash.

Lover Boy doubled over and deposited his lunch between us. I jumped back to avoid the splatter. His two buddies stared, puzzled by what had happened, their eyes decoyed by my right hand.

As Lover Boy struggled to catch his breath, I leaned in, and in a whisper, I said, "Gosh, you don't look so good. Must've been something you said."

I turned away and sauntered off to class. I'd won my first challenge, two weeks shy of my fourteenth birthday.

The rest of my night shift passed without further incident. After I briefed the day clerks on the events of my shift, skimming over the incident with Funny George and Fuck You, I drove my aged Volkswagen Beetle to the South Miami police station. Sunset Drive is quiet at that time of the morning, and I had no problem getting there or finding a parking space.

As I walked towards the entrance door, I caught sight of a heart-shaped stone memorial on the left side of the entrance. It bore the photograph of a man named Officer Schulz, who'd lost his life in the line of duty. Out of habit, I paused and finger-saluted Officer Schulz's picture.

I moved through to the reception counter and explained to the duty officer I was there to see Officer Jackson. I was told to have a seat and he'd page him. I had time to sit down and glance at the dog-eared magazine selection before Officer Jackson appeared.

"Thanks for coming in," he said, all business. "This way, please."

I fell in step behind him and followed through a door secured by a key pad. He led the way to an interview room. It was sparsely furnished with four chairs, two on either side of a metal table. The chairs and table, I noted, were bolted to the concrete floor. Made it tough for unruly suspects to raise hell.

"Lieutenant Marco Lopez will be joining us," Jackson told me.

Another man came through the door, then closed it behind him. As he walked towards me, I sized him up. Late thirties, five ten or so, solid build, rugged, chiseled features, wearing standard blues. He radiated self-confidence. He held a manila folder in his left hand.

He extended his right hand to me while confirming he was Lieutenant Lopez, head of the robbery division.

"EZ Kelly, sir," I said, taking his hand and returning his firm shake.

"Thanks for your cooperation, Miss Kelly." He circled the table and took the chair by Officer Jackson.

"Always ready to do my civic duty," I replied, smiling.

"Wish everyone felt that way." He opened the folder and spread several papers before him.

"Officer Jackson tells me you subdued these two subjects all by your lonesome. Is that correct?" He raised an eyebrow as he asked the question.

"Yes, sir. That's right."

"Do you mind telling me where you got the training to do that?"

"Not at all. My father taught me. He was a Green Beret, Special Forces. He thought I should know how to defend myself, especially after he and Mom named me EZ. Said he couldn't guarantee that he'd always be there for me, so he taught me what he knew to help me stay safe."

"Seems he taught you well, young lady," Lieutenant Lopez said, a grin turning up the corners of his mouth.

I nodded. "He did indeed, sir. He started teaching me while I was still in diapers, and whenever I see him we'll spar together."

"Hell of a father," Lopez quipped.

"Yes, sir."

Lieutenant Lopez set a tape recorder on the table between us, and pushed RECORD. "I'd like you to go over in detail the incident that occurred at the Adriatic Hotel early this morning. For the record," he added, pointing at the tape recorder.

"Sure." I collected my thoughts, then launched into a review of my encounter with the two would-be thieves, taking my time to think back and give a thorough account of the timeline. Finished, I said, "Guess that's it, sir."

"Thanks, Miss Kelly. That will do nicely. Now, a couple questions about you," continued the Lieutenant. "We have your name as EZ Kelly, twenty-eight-years old, from Columbia, South Carolina. Do you have an address in the Miami area?"

"I do, sir." I gave it to him and he wrote it down.

"What brought you to the Adriatic Hotel in South Beach?"

"I'm working at becoming a travel agent. I've taken the course work, and now I'm doing on-the-job training."

"So, working behind the desk in a hotel gets you to be a travel agent?" asked Lopez, a skeptical expression on his face.

"It's one way," I said, as I considered the convoluted path I'd chosen. "A lot of people want to be travel agents, but if you want to make enough money at it to support yourself, you have to climb the ladder. My goal is to move from the front desk to the travel desk. From there, I'm hoping for a position in a travel agency." I shrugged my shoulders. "Working as a hotel desk clerk is the first rung on the ladder for me."

"What's another way?" probed the Lieutenant.

"Know someone in a travel agency who takes you under their wing, teaches you the ropes, gives you the opportunity to make or break it. I don't have any contacts like that, so I'm a desk clerk for now," I explained.

"Got it," said Lieutenant Lopez. "Good luck with that."

"Thanks."

"Now, there's one more thing you should know," began Lopez. "The two men you incapacitated and got arrested, they have no prior records that we could find. They're facing charges of attempted armed robbery, and in one case, illegal possession of a firearm. Not real serious charges. My guess, knowing how the judicial system works, is they'll get slaps on the wrist, told to behave themselves, and get cut loose. Maybe they'll serve a couple months, but I'd be surprised, given how crowded our jails and prisons are.

"The reason why I'm telling you this is I think you should consider the possibility that these two thugs might come after you when they're back out again, try to even the score, so to speak. We, the police department, that is, don't have the resources to protect you from them, sorry to have to tell you. So maybe you should consider moving, getting a job behind the desk in another city, another part of the country."

I shook my head no. I wasn't afraid to stand up to these men again. "That's not going to work for me. My dad taught me that for every action there's an equal and opposite reaction. Running from this isn't a solution. I can be looking over my shoulder in Miami, or in Timbuktu. I prefer Miami."

"Your decision," said Lopez. "Tell you what. I'll get the word to you when these birds are freed. That way, you'll at least have a heads-up."

"Thanks. I appreciate that, sir. So are we done here? It's past my bedtime." I stifled a yawn.

"We are. Thanks for your cooperation. Oh, and EZ. Wish we had more people like you out there. Makes our job a lot easier, no pun intended," joked Lieutenant Lopez, standing up.

I got to my feet, and after good-bye handshakes, I headed out the door. Once in my car, I made tracks for my apartment, which lay well outside the high rent district.

My building has sixteen apartments, four to a floor, four stories tall. I parked on the street, which at that hour of the morning was made easier by day workers vacating their spaces. It worked well for me, day after day.

My apartment is on the third floor, facing the street. I can look down and check on my parked Beetle, though my old VW isn't one of the more desirable cars to steal, especially in its condition. My living quarters aren't fancy. There's a small bedroom, a combination living room/kitchen/dining nook, and a snug bathroom with a stall shower. It suits me fine. No frills. Solid deadbolt on the door. Safe.

I locked the door behind me and kicked off my shoes. Next I unbuttoned my blouse and shrugged out of my pants. Reduced to bra and panties, I moved directly into my exercise routine of kicks, jabs, pivots, and leaps, shaking off the effects of eight hours at a boring job, with the minor interruption.

After twenty minutes of my fast-paced routine I stopped, took five minutes to stretch out my humming muscles, then dropped my panties and bra into the hamper.

I padded into the bathroom and turned on the shower. While I waited for the water to turn warm, I ran my hands over my body, feeling its firmness, then trailed my fingers down over my flat, muscular stomach. I liked my body. It had never betrayed me.

The water now warm, I stepped into the shower. I grabbed my loofa and creamy body wash and soaped up, running the loofa over my muscular body. Then I rinsed off the accumulations of the last sixteen hours, letting the warm water wash over me.

I shut off the shower and reached for the thick towel, letting my hair drip dry.

Soon after, I crawled into my double bed and pulled the sheet over me. With my mind still humming along despite my fatigue, I ran a series of possibilities to explain what Funny George and Fuck You had come for at the hotel. Money was way down on my list of possibilities. Something else was going on here. I felt it in my bones.

Chapter Two

Day Two

My next night on the job started at eleven, as usual. Most of the guests had retired to their rooms, leaving me alone to tend to the few who drifted in later. Management, in their wisdom, had one desk clerk on from eleven to seven. It saved them another salary, and most of the time, it worked out fine.

I've considered reading a book during the dead period of my shift, but the ever-present camera trained on me and the counter is a constant reminder it could work against me when talk of advancement comes up. So I keep busy by straightening up the counter, placing pens in the cup holder, and moving the register about to make it more accessible. Lots of stupid little stuff to give me something to do, makes the time slide by, like checking to make sure the registration computer monitor is directed away from prying eyes. Still, all this takes ten, fifteen minutes, tops, if I stretch it. Checking for dust bunnies is next.

Once I have the counter neat and straightened, I exit the front desk enclosure via the door and start on the tour information desk. Set in an open area of the lobby, it invites guests to explore all the possible tours they could take in the Miami Beach area and beyond.

As I sit behind the desk and pick up the brochures that describe each tour, I read each one in detail, then picture myself explaining each tour to an interested guest. It's my next step up the ladder to becoming a travel agent.

I made the decision to become a travel agent during my second year of college. I'd gone to a jobs fair, and had been intrigued by the presentation of a representative of the American Society of Travel Agents. She'd emphasized all the perks of the occupation, hitting on the biggest one: free travel trips to all the resorts and cities around the world.

"After all," she'd said with a sly smile, "how could you recommend a place to a customer if you haven't been there yourself?"

The thought of exploring the world and having it paid for by a resort or a chamber of commerce anxious to have their location promoted had serious appeal. I was hooked.

Somebody pushed the lobby door open, snapping me back to the present with a start.

I got up and hurried back to the front desk while keeping track of the young man moving rapidly towards me. I watched him sweep the lobby with his eyes as he advanced to the counter.

When I reached the front desk entry door, I turned to face him. He smiled, asked if there were any rooms available.

"Yes, sir. You're in luck," I said, returning his smile.

"Oh, great!" he said, his athletic face showing relief.

I turned to punch the four-digit door code into the keypad. As I pulled the door open, the man hauled a handgun from his jacket pocket and leveled it at my face.

"Get in there and open the safe!" he ordered, his smile gone.

Here we go again.

I eased inside the front desk enclosure, wondering if this guy and last night's bozo went through the same training program. I was prodded forward by the intent young man. His gun hand never wavered. He spotted the safe under the counter, pointed at it and ordered me to open it.

"Please don't hurt me!" I begged him, using what I hoped sounded like the panicked voice of a frightened young woman. My heart picked up its pace with anticipation.

"Just do it!" he snarled.

I turned away from him and bent down towards the safe. He made the mistake of standing too close behind me. I pretended to lose my balance and stumbled to my left.

It distracted him, as I'd hoped.

I pivoted on my left hand and drove my right foot into his midsection. The sudden impact drove his body backwards with such force that he flew into the wall with a shuddering crash, his handgun falling from his hand.

I caught the gun before it hit the floor. He shook his head to clear it, then found himself staring down the barrel of his own gun.

I ordered him to hit the deck, clasp his hands behind his head. He hesitated for an instant, then complied.

I secured him with twine, same as I'd done the night before. Satisfied with my handiwork, I left him lying there and walked to the lobby door. Looking out, I could see a car parked there, exhaust spilling from the tailpipe, the passenger door hanging open.

Time to let the police earn their keep. I walked to the front desk and called 9-1-1. After explaining the situation to the dispatcher, I requested they send two cruisers, hold the lights and sirens, so they could move in silently to block and apprehend the driver in the getaway car.

While waiting for the police to arrive, I reviewed the events of the past two nights. Though robbery could be the motive, I sensed something else at play here.

My thoughts were interrupted by the screeching tires of two cruisers pulling in to block the getaway car and driver. Loud voices shouting commands at the surprised driver carried in to me, and then there was silence. The lobby door swung wide and Officer Jackson and his partner strode in, hands on sidearms. They were both on high alert. His partner hung back, making it impossible to see his name tag.

"Well, well! Miss Kelly again," he said, tension draining from him. "What the hell's going on?" He'd spotted me standing by the front desk.

"You tell me, Officer," I said in a calm, relaxed manner.

"You got another one waiting behind the counter?"

"Guilty," I answered, a coy smile playing across my face.

"Same scenario as last night?" he asked.

"Pretty much the same."

"That'll save us all some time. Was he armed?"

"Yes. Handgun looks to be similar to the one used last night. Let me show you." I led the way into the front desk enclosure, pointed down at the perpetrator, then toward the handgun on the desk. Officer Jackson dealt with the gun first. After pulling on a pair of latex gloves, he dumped the magazine and ejected the round from the chamber, dropping each item into an evidence bag held out by his partner. Finished, he bent down and helped the would-be thief to his feet, handcuffed his hands behind his back, then removed my twine cuffs.

He steered the man to the front entrance, then turned back to me. "Let's all save ourselves a little time. See you at the station when you get off." An order, delivered in a neutral manner.

"I'll be there. Thanks, Officer Jackson."

His expression said he was surprised I remembered his name. Surprised in a nice way. With a parting half-smile, he left, guiding the trussed up would-be thief ahead of him.

Once the cruisers had left with their two-man cargoes, I busied myself with a brief cleanup, which consisted of picking up the twine pieces from the floor and making a visual inspection of the area. Maintenance would need to make minor repairs to the sheet rock wall. Again.

Not long after, the police tow truck pulled up in front. They hooked onto the getaway car and hauled it off to impound.

A glance at the clock told me I had three hours to kill before shift change. The mild adrenaline rush from the set-to with the armed man would keep me awake until then.

I reviewed the events of the past two nights, and concluded that this job was anything but dull. If this keeps up, maybe I should request hazardous duty pay. The thought made me laugh out loud.

Once again, with time to kill, I found myself recalling another obnoxious high school boy. I'd made the girls' soccer team my sophomore year, and all the practice sessions Dad put me through gave me better balance and coordination. I was center forward, and became good at getting passes, dodging past defenders, and burying the ball in the back of the net.

We had a regular cheering section, plus a few football jocks who showed up to look us and acted obnoxious as we played. We joked about them in the shower after the games.

One afternoon a couple of us stepped out of the locker room and one of the *peepers*, that's what we called them, stood outside, waiting. He sauntered up to meet us.

"Nice game, ladies," Mister Peeper said to us.

We ignored him, kept walking.

He crowded in next to me, displacing one of my friends. "Well hey, EZ. What say we go somewhere and get better acquainted?"

I turned to face him. "Why should I do that?"

"That's easy, EZ. I'm easy, and I'm guessing you are, too," he said, using a line that was obviously well-rehearsed.

"You make it *easy* for me to say no. There's nothing easy about me," I said, my face serious.

My friends had stopped, surrounding us, eager to see the outcome.

Mister Peeper, undaunted, went on the offensive. He draped an arm over my shoulder and began guiding me away from my friends.

"Take your hands off me, please," I asked him in my gentlest voice.

"Oh, that's so hard to do. My arm feels right at home there." He punctuated this with what I guessed was his best smile.

"Let me help you," I said.

I grabbed the pinkie of his offending hand and bent it in a direction it was never meant to go. When I felt a pop, I released it.

"Ow, ow, ow! Jesus!" He brought his hand before his eyes, shocked at the new angle his pinkie had taken.

Dislocated fingers are seriously painful, and they remain so until put back in place.

"Ooh! What have you done?" I asked, trying to sound sympathetic as I reached for his hand.

"You did that!" he wailed and began to tremble. Distracted, he was unaware of me grabbing his pinkie with one hand and the bulk of his hand in the other. I gave a vigorous yank outward until I felt the pop again.

That got his attention. He examined his hand again, saw his pinkie was back where it belonged. I knew the pain lived on, but it'd been reduced a lot when I made the adjustment.

I turned to my friends. "Did you see me do anything?" I asked them in my most innocent voice.

"No," they replied as one, smiled as one.

Not long after that, word got out that I was rumored to be a lesbian. It spread through school like a tidal wave. I ignored it. Those who wanted to believe, believed. Those who didn't, didn't. Two girls asked me if it was true. I told them it wasn't. That ended it. I never knew if they were curious, or maybe fishing.

My shift ended, and I drove to the police station. Officer Jackson met me as I walked in, and Lieutenant Lopez joined us soon after. We used the same interrogation room, sat in the same seats.

"This is getting to be a habit, Miss Kelly," Lieutenant Lopez began. "What the hell's going on?"

"You want my honest opinion, sir? I don't think it's money they're after."

"Yeah? What then?" Lopez shot back.

I shrugged my shoulders. "I don't know. Maybe they're after

something left there for safekeeping by a hotel guest."

Lopez leaned back in his chair, considering. After a moment of silence, he sat forward again, fixing me with his eyes. "You know, you may be right," he admitted. "Let's go have a looksee."

"My manager gets in at eight. And knowing him, he'll want to see a warrant."

Lieutenant Lopez gave Jackson a sideways glance. "Go ahead and tape her statement. I'll get the warrant." He stood and left the room.

Officer Jackson set a tape recorder between us, pushed RECORD, and stated the date and time. He said he was Officer Andrew Jackson, then stated my name and a brief description of the facts. Then he asked me to elaborate on the events of the past six hours.

I did so.

Finished, I said, "I guess that's it."

Jackson reached forward and turned off the recorder.

I cocked my head to one side, and asked, "Andrew Jackson. Really? Friends call you 'Stonewall'?"

"No. It's Andy," he replied a little too quickly, color flooding his face.

"Looks like your parents had a little fun with *your* name, too."

"That they did. Guess we're members of the same club," he ventured, returning my smile.

"Yes, and stronger because of it," I added.

The door opened, and Lieutenant Lopez stuck his head in. "If you're done, let's go. I got the warrant."

Jackson and I followed Lopez out to the parking lot. We climbed into his unmarked cruiser and he drove us to the Adriatic Hotel.

When we stepped into the lobby, we drew several curious stares. I walked up to the counter and, in a hushed voice, explained to the manager what the police were there for. He accepted the warrant, glanced briefly at it, then opened the door. Andy and I remained on the outer side of the counter while Lopez went behind the counter.

The manager opened the safe, then stepped back.

Lieutenant Lopez bent down and removed each item from the safe, placing them on the desktop in a neat row. Jackson kept inquisitive onlookers from approaching the counter while Lopez worked. I had a clear view of all the items Lopez took out, and looked everything over as he held them in his hands.

The items ran the gamut. There were envelopes containing cash, bags containing jewelry, and larger envelopes that held a variety of documents which were too far away for me to decipher. Lopez spread the documents on the counter and photographed each one with his cell phone for closer examination later.

One particular item caught my eye. A large gold ID bracelet sat amongst several other pieces of men's jewelry Lopez had dumped from a bag. Its size drew my attention. It had to be the largest ID bracelet I'd ever seen. I pictured a giant of a man wearing it. Then my eyes swept over the other jewelry. Even at that distance I could see that the rings were, if anything, smaller than expected.

Strange.

Lopez finished his examination, then carefully replaced each item in the safe.

He turned to the manager. "Thank you, sir. We're done here. The South Miami Police Department appreciates your cooperation." He punctuated his words by reaching out and shaking the manager's hand.

He stepped out into the lobby, his long strides a signal to Officer Jackson and me that he had finished his search. We trailed him outside and climbed back into his cruiser for the trip to the station.

"Did you find anything?" I asked, once we were on our way.

"I won't know until we review each of the documents I photographed," he told me. "If anything turns up, I'll let you know."

"Thanks. I appreciate that."

"By the way, Miss Kelly. As you no doubt know, this is now four unhappy would-be thieves who will likely be out on the street much too soon. You sure you don't want to reconsider a move to a safer city, a safer situation?"

"No, sir. I'll be sticking to my guns right here in sunny Miami," I said.

"I hope that turns out to be a wise decision."

I could hear the concern come through in his professional voice. It gave me a small degree of comfort.

We rode the rest of the way to the station in silence, each of us immersed in our own thoughts. Lopez parked his cruiser next to my VW, his way of saying 'thank you' for my time and trouble, I suppose.

I exited his cruiser, said good-bye to Jackson and Lopez, and pointed my VW towards home.

Once there, I followed my usual routine: twenty minutes of strenuous exercise, five minutes to stretch, then a hot shower.

As I lay in bed, I considered the two nights of attempted robberies and the unusual ID bracelet. *What the hell. Might as well have a look at it tomorrow. Might help solve the mystery.*

Chapter Three

Day Three

The next night when I arrived for work, my manager was there to greet me. Dressed in a dark suit, solid tie, hair flawlessly combed, he smiled at me as I approached the counter.

"Hello, Miss Kelly. I came in to see if you might want someone else to be with you during your shift, especially after what's happened here the past two nights."

His offer came as such a surprise to me, I didn't know what to say. I recovered quickly. "That's very kind of you, sir, but I'm okay working alone. I think it was a coincidence that two attempts to rob the hotel safe were made two nights in a row." As I spoke, I assessed his physical condition. Soft, muscles gone to flab, hands manicured for show, not defense. He would be more of an obstacle than a helping hand if trouble came calling again.

Hearing my words, he visibly relaxed, clearly relieved that he didn't need to stay, maybe face some unexpected danger. "Well, Miss Kelly, if you're sure you'll be okay working by yourself after what's happened to you the last two nights—"

I interrupted him. "I'm sure, sir. Thank you for thinking about me and making the offer. I truly appreciate it." I tried to reassure him I'd be fine on my own.

"It's the least I could do, under the circumstances. If you're absolutely certain that you'll be okay working here by yourself—"

"I am, sir," I cut him off.

"Well, then, very good, Miss Kelly. I'll leave you to your duties." He whistled a happy tune as he exited the hotel lobby.

Once the lobby door closed behind him, I breathed a sigh of relief. I'd learned over the years that certain people shouldn't be around during a firefight. I was sure he was one of them.

A short time later, a registering guest gave me the excuse needed to open the safe. If I'd opened it without having cash or a credit card receipt to put inside, it could raise questions when the surveillance tape got reviewed. I didn't need that.

I crouched down in front of the safe, using my body to block the camera's view, and entered the six-digit code, then swung the door open.

After tucking the credit card receipt in the appropriate envelope, I found the pouch of jewelry, opened it and pulled out the ID bracelet. Despite its size, it felt surprisingly light. Turning it over, I noticed a fine seam near one end. I grasped it on the two sides and pulled. The bracelet separated, revealing the end of a carefully hidden flash drive.

Interesting. What have we got here?

Taking care to conceal the camera's view of the bracelet, I closed the safe and stood up. A quick glance around reassured me I was alone, the lobby empty. I strolled casually to the tour reservations desk, sat down and fired up the computer. Once up and running, I inserted the flash drive bracelet into an open USB port and followed the screen prompts to download the data.

It took less than a minute. I removed the flash drive, put the bracelet together once again, then opened the file, feeling a minor pang of guilt for violating a guest's privacy.

What came up on the screen made no sense to me. There were three lines. Dates and times, with GPS coordinates displayed in degrees and minutes next to each date. I saw that the degrees and minutes were all within two or three miles of each other. The times were scattered, but all occurred during the night hours. The dates covered slightly less than a week, the first one being three nights away, later this week.

I considered sharing the information with Detective Lopez. Making a copy made sense.

I switched on the copy machine and hit the PRINT key once. It hummed and spit out a single sheet of paper with the crazy dates, times, and locations arranged in a nice column. Lots of free space on the paper. Lots of wasted paper if you're a tree hugger. Then I had another idea.

I searched the desk drawers and found a three-pack of new flash drives. Removing one, I stuck it into the computer USB port, then transferred the skimpy file onto it. Once finished, I deleted the file from the tour desk computer, turned it and the printer off, and returned to the front desk.

I realized I needed one more piece of information: the name of the person who left the jewelry in the safe. That would more than likely be on a piece of paper inside the jewelry bag.

Now I needed to wait for a reason to open the safe, put the bracelet back, and find the owner's name.

The reason strolled into the lobby less than forty-five minutes later. Nearly six feet tall, he had a solid frame and moved with confidence. He had his right hand tucked inside his windbreaker pocket. *What's with all the windbreakers? Miami's warm enough, day or night, regardless of the time of year.*

I had a hunch.

What the hell. This is crazy. Could this be Round Three? I followed his progress as he made his way across the empty lobby towards the check-in counter.

He sauntered up to me, smiling the whole while, then damned if he didn't pull a compact semiautomatic pistol from his windbreaker pocket and level it at my head.

I stepped back, allowed my mouth to drop open in apparent shock, then whimpered "Please! Don't hurt me!" in my most pathetic voice.

"Do as I say and you won't get hurt. Now open the safe!"

I moved to do his bidding, and the man vaulted the counter, landing directly behind me on the balls of his feet.

I bent down, entered the combination, then pulled open the safe door. Done, I stood up and moved back, allowing the man access.

"Stand over there!" he ordered.

I moved where he indicated, realizing it gave him a clear shot at me while he explored the safe. I guessed he had some training, or maybe he blundered into being lucky. I watched him sort through the safe's contents, then pull out the black velour jewelry bag and dump its contents on the floor in front of him. He separated the various pieces, then mumbled, "Where is it?" Frustration was evident in his voice.

"Where is what?" I asked, trying my best to sound nervous, scared.

"Shut up!" he shouted at me.

I shut up, but continued to watch his every move. I saw my opening when he took his eyes off me to search the scattered jewelry on the floor. My turn to take command.

Using a move I'd practiced hundreds of times, I drove my right heel into his exposed right shoulder, rocketing him forward. The steel safe door interrupted the forward progress of his head with a satisfying crack. He slumped to the floor, unconscious.

Seeing how soundly he slept, I decided not to waste my time tying him up. I retrieved his handgun and set it on the desk, then picked up the desk phone and called 9-1-1. I told the dispatcher what had happened, and asked her to send two cruisers, just like last night, leave off the lights and sirens, no sense giving the driver waiting outside time to exit stage right.

There was a brief pause while the dispatcher reviewed last night's log, I'm guessing, and said, "Oh, yeah. Ten-four. Will do."

With my back blocking the ever-present camera's view of the safe, I crouched down and dropped the ID bracelet onto the pile of jewelry the would-be thief had left on the floor. I felt inside the bag and located the card identifying the bag's owner, slipped it out, read it, committed it to memory. Then I tucked it back in the empty bag and stood up. The whole sequence took me less than thirty seconds. I could feel my heart pounding the entire time.

Soon after, the cruisers showed up without any fanfare, blocking the exit of what I assumed was the getaway car, and two officers rushed into the lobby, hands tight on holsters. One was Officer Andrew Jackson. He smiled when he saw me waiting casually by the desk counter.

"Hello again, EZ. Is there a perp behind the counter?"

"There is," I said, my voice calm. "You know, Officer Jackson, we've got to stop meeting like this." I grinned.

"You got that right," he agreed, returning my smile.

I opened the passage door and let Andy Jackson and his partner through. Name tag said he was Robert Lee. Another confederate namesake? About then the would-be thief began showing signs of life. Jackson stood the man up and handcuffed his hands behind his back, then turned his attention to the handgun. His gloved hands removed the loaded magazine and ejected the cartridge from the chamber while Robert Lee bagged it all.

"Same scenario as the other two?" asked Andy.

"Almost. This time I opened the safe for him. I was curious about what he came for."

"What did he come for?"

"That bag of jewelry you see on the floor. He pawed through it, then said 'Where is it?' just before I slammed his head into the side of the safe. I have no idea what he came for."

While Jackson took out his cell phone and took a picture of the scattered jewelry, the would-be thief glanced down at the same time. If anyone had been watching him, they would have seen his mouth drop open, his eyebrows arch in surprise. As it turned out, only I noticed his reaction.

"So's you know," said Jackson, "we apprehended the driver waiting outside, just like the other two. This is starting to take on the appearance of an endless loop tape," he said drily.

"You're right. It's made my last three nights a lot more interesting, but I have to admit, I could do without it. I wouldn't mind a boring night."

"I'm sure. Don't forget to come in after your shift to give your testimony," he reminded me.

"Yeah, yeah. Take another hour off my sleep schedule. That hurts the most," I said with a shake of my head.

"Sorry about that. See you around seven." Officers Jackson and Lee escorted the prisoner out to their idling cruiser.

After they left, I turned to the task of cleaning up the mess left behind. I crouched down, this time positioning myself so the camera had an unobstructed view of what I was doing. Satisfied, I scooped up the items of jewelry scattered on the floor in front of the safe, dropping them one by one back in the velour bag. The ID bracelet went in last.

Finished, I pulled the drawstring to close the bag, then set it inside the safe and closed the door. I turned the handle, locking it once again.

I stood up, stretching my shoulder and back muscles as I did so, and moved behind the small desk within the enclosure. Once again, the sounds of the police tow truck doing its thing with getaway car number three filled the hotel lobby.

I sat down, considering what I should do with the flash drive copy I'd made. Turn it over to the police? What about the owner's name I'd memorized? And what the hell made it so interesting that three different attempts were made to steal the information on the flash drive?

I didn't doubt for a second that all three attempts were connected. They had to be. Once, okay. Twice, maybe. Three times? No doubt.

Still not sure what to do with the flash drive, I decided I'd make a decision once I got to the police station. Meanwhile, there'd be time to mull it over, maybe think of something I'd missed along the way. Dad had hammered home to me not to make quick decisions without having all the facts. This might be one of those times.

After going over my night's activities, and being razzed by the morning staff for another crazy night on the job, I drove to the South Miami police station. I parked alongside Lieutenant Lopez's cruiser and made my way to the reception counter.

I found myself smiling at the differences between this counter and the one at the Adriatic. Then, thinking about my last three nights there, I figured maybe the differences weren't as great as I'd first thought.

Officer Andrew Jackson stood by the counter, clearly waiting for me. He smiled, seeing me. "Come on, EZ. Let's get this done so you can get some sleep."

I noticed that I was on a first-name basis with him.

"Lead the way, Andy," I said, using his first name.

I followed him to the same interview room. Lieutenant Lopez sat waiting for us.

"Hi, Lieutenant. Learn anything from the documents and stuff from the safe?" I asked as I slid into the chair across from him.

"Nothing so far. I've sent them off to forensics for a thorough going-over," he said.

I tapped my finger on the table. "What about the six would-be thieves? There must be a connection," I pressed.

He shrugged. "I'm stumped. Our preliminary search of data banks has turned up nothing. None of the men have priors, none come up anywhere."

"Sounds like someone's gone to a lot of trouble to get something from that safe, even picking players who can't be traced. Have any of the six men told you anything?"

"They're well-rehearsed. To a man, they're telling the same story. They needed money, figured a hotel safe would be an easy knock-off, and it's a coincidence that they all happened to pick the Adriatic Hotel. Yeah, right! Try as we might, we couldn't get any of them to change their story," Lopez concluded.

"So what's your gut tell you?" Jackson asked.

At this point, I think Lopez felt my piercing blue eyes on his.

"I'm thinking there's two possibilities. Maybe it's a well-organized gang that's after something, who knows what," said Lopez.

"Or?" I asked.

"Yeah. Or it's some federal deal, who knows? Maybe Homeland

Security, DEA, or ICE. Could be any one of them, plus a bunch more," Lopez conceded.

"Have any of the men you've got in custody got lawyers, or had anyone reach out to them?"

"That's the funny thing. None of them have made an attempt to get a lawyer, make that one phone call they're all entitled to. They sit together in the holding cell and stare at their hands, twiddle their thumbs, don't even talk to each other. They act like a bunch of strangers. No, that's not true. Strangers would talk a little, break the ice, show some curiosity. These guys ignore each other. Never seen anything like it," Lopez admitted, spreading his hands on the table between us.

I thought of the flash drive, wondered if it could offer information that would bring light to all this confusion. It felt good knowing it was hidden safely away at the Adriatic, knowing I could put my hands on it at any time, pass it on to Lopez if it seemed right. But now didn't seem like the right time. I don't know why, but I've learned to trust my instincts.

"Strange," I murmured.

"You got that right." Then Lopez changed direction. First, he reminded me that there were now six men who could make life miserable for me when they got out, and didn't I want to reconsider leaving Miami for some place safer? Why was I getting the feeling that Lopez wanted me far, far away?

I told him not to worry, I could take care of myself. Lopez conceded that I had a right to my choice. Then he turned to Jackson, told him to finish the interview. "I'm sure Miss Kelly wants to get out of here," he added, smiling at me.

Officer Jackson, all business, got right to the task of recording my testimony, which was eerily similar to the two before this one. The only variant was the manner in which I'd taken the men down.

When he finished, Andy Jackson turned off the tape recorder and said, "Maybe you and I could meet at the gym some time, you could show me some of your moves."

I considered him carefully. *Was he coming on to me?* No. He was serious. I looked him in the eye and said, "Hey, why not? I could use a sparring partner."

"Hope you don't mean a punching bag," he countered, grinning.

I laughed, and felt the stress of the night lift away. "Nope."

***

The drive home was without incident. By that time in the morning, the traffic going in my direction had thinned, and I got home without delay. I parked on the street, locked my car, and used my key to open the entrance door. Even though the building had an elevator, I preferred to climb the two flights of stairs. It got me there faster, and I liked the exercise.

With my mind preoccupied by the contents of the flash drive, I keyed the lock to my apartment and pushed the door open. Then an *uh oh* feeling hit me. A different smell, maybe.

Before I could put it together, an arm shot out from behind the door. I felt a jolt, a crackling sensation, and all my muscles betrayed me. I dropped to the floor, awake, aware, but unable to move.

I knew what had happened. I'd been shocked by a stun gun. I silently cursed my carelessness. My eyes, the one thing I *could* move, swept the space before me, saw a pair of feet, a man's, uglier than hell. I memorized them. It was all I could do.

A man's hands searched every possible hiding place in my pantsuit, patting me down. Then he hauled my pants down to my ankles and probed my body, felt every crevice, every possible hiding place, and then, pushed groping fingers into my body, penetrating and searching. I felt violated and wanted to fight back. All I could do was lay where I fell.

I knew what he was looking for. He thought I had the ID bracelet with the secret flash drive. He checked every hiding place I might've used, then went back and checked them all again. I knew one thing for sure: this man had earned himself the privilege of a slow, agonizing death. I hoped I'd have the opportunity down the road.

He finished his search and stepped back. I still couldn't see his face, but I could feel his anger. Anger and frustration.

He moved in close to me and hauled my arms roughly behind my back. I heard a rapid clicking sound. Zip tie. He'd immobilized me against the time when I'd regain the use of my muscles. I recalled what I knew of stun guns, the length of time it disabled a victim, remembered that the effects lasted around a minute. That is, unless the shock is applied again.

My mind regained control of my muscles, but I continued to act limp, unresponsive, hoping to avoid a second shock.

My assailant grabbed my arms and lifted me up, then positioned me with my back against the wall. I pretended I had no control over my muscles, allowed my torso to slide along the wall and back to the floor. As I did so, I got a good look at my assailant. Thirties, tall and lean, close-cropped black hair, broad, hard face, and dressed casually. His shoes, uglier than hell, held my attention. Neon green and gold. Garish. Probably cost him a month's rent.

I saw a second man, too, standing back watching the show, with a bored expression on his Hispanic face.

"Still a little fuzzy, huh?" my assailant said. "While you're coming around, maybe you'd like to tell me where the flash drive is."

"Flash drive?" I purposely slurred my words, doing my best to sound like I didn't know what he meant. His accent puzzled me.

"Don't play dumb, girl! We know you got your hands on the ID bracelet. Our man saw it on the floor after you knocked him out. Said it wasn't there before you hit him."

"Oh, that," I mumbled. "After he got knocked out, I felt around under the safe and found it. I heard him say, 'Where is it?' and got curious about what he meant. A gold ID bracelet, right?"

The man stared at me, confusion dominating his face. Then his features hardened. "I find out you're lying, you're dead," he snarled at me, stabbing the air in front of my face with his blunt index finger. He turned to his accomplice and gave him a 'Let's go' wave and they headed for the door.

"Aren't you going to cut me loose?" I asked, working a little concern into my voice.

"Go to hell! Get your own ass out of it!"

Then they were gone.

His accent sounded Central American, maybe once removed.

Getting out of the zip tie bonds took no time at all. Dad had shown me how to pull my bound hands under my butt and down the back of my legs, then tuck my feet through the loop. That brought my hands in front. That accomplished, I went to the kitchen counter, partially withdrew one of the knives from the knife block, and slipped the handle behind the zip tie. Standing behind it, I pulled backward against the blade, cutting the tie and releasing my hands.

Freed, I rushed to the front window and looked out in time to spot the two men driving off in a large black sedan. I couldn't make out the license plate or see any other identifying marks. The driver tapped the brakes when they turned the corner, and I noticed the left rear brake light was out. I tucked that away in my memory banks.

I turned away from the window and, on autopilot, I checked the locks on the door to make sure they were secured. Next thing I needed to do was wash away the filth left behind by the creep's probing fingers. I stripped out of my soiled clothing and stood, trembling, while the shower water turned warm. Then I stepped under the soothing stream and let it flow over my violated body, allowing it to wash away the lingering effects of the painful probings I'd endured.

I soaped my body from head to toe, and rinsed it all off. The memory of the invasive assault clung to me like hot mud. I soaped my body again, working the foam into my deepest recesses, and allowed the soap's fragrance to reach into and soothe my mind. Despite all my efforts, I still felt dirty.

I switched gears. I stepped from the shower, toweled off, and began my exercise routine. I stepped into my kicks, lunges and punches, each one directed at my mind's image of the creep who'd violated me. I moved slowly at first because of the lingering effects of the stun gun, but finishing strong, the creep's face strong in my mind. Then I showered again, taking extra time, allowing the water to wash away the lingering effects of the violation I'd endured.

It wasn't enough. I still felt so dirty. I knew the shower alone wouldn't erase the memory.

With the water growing cold, I shut it off and stepped out. I picked up my damp towel and dried myself. Done and dry, I sat on the edge of the bed, picked up the phone, and punched in a familiar number.

The person on the other end answered on the second ring. "Kelly," came the terse response.

"Hey, Dad."

"Hey, EZ! What's wrong? Are you okay? I hear sadness and a lot of anger in your voice."

"You know me too well, Dad."

"Tell me," he prompted.

I'd always been closer to Dad than Mom, so I did. I started my story with the three attempted robberies and my responses, ending with the search done on me. I wasn't one to show vulnerabilities, but this had cut me to the core. Then, having to tell my father I'd been assaulted. A tear slipped down my face, and I quickly swept it away. *No way that creep can control my reaction!*

Dad listened without interruption. When I'd finished, he said, "I'm sorry you had to go through that. It could've been a lot worse."

I got what he meant. Flat on the floor, no control over my body, a man looming over me. Yes, it could have been worse. It was bad enough— an experience I had no desire to ever repeat. "Yeah, you're right."

While we talked, another inconsistency welled up in my head. I told Dad that the detective told me none of the prisoners had requested lawyers, none said a word, none had any outside contacts. If that was true, how'd the asshole who stunned and searched me know who I was or what happened six hours before? There must've been communication with the third guy I whacked, the one who opened the jewelry pouch looking for the ID bracelet.

"Sharp observation, Ease. Be careful with those cops. Might be a bad apple in there."

I cocked my head to the side, still wondering. "Yeah. As you know, *Careful* is my middle name."

"It's a good one. So, what's the deal with the bracelet?"

I told him, beginning with my suspicions because of its size, then noticing the seam in it, and finally pulling it apart to reveal the flash drive. I reviewed how I'd downloaded the file on the hotel computer, then made a copy of it before putting it back in the safe.

"What's in the file?" he asked, getting right to the point.

"Three different dates and times, with map coordinates next to each entry."

"Did you check where the coordinates are located?"

I frowned. "Not yet, but I will."

"It may tell you something," he went on, his voice even, non-judgmental. "That is, if you still have the flash drive copy."

"I do. I put it back in the three-pack I took it from, in the tour desk. I thought it'd be safer there than carrying it with me."

"Good call, Ease. If they'd found it on you, things might've turned out different."

I got his point. Dead, is what he meant. "I know, Dad. I got lucky."

"No, you know damned well you didn't get lucky. You used your smarts, you used your head, and you followed your instincts. Luck has nothing to do with it. You start betting on luck, you'll lose every time."

I laughed, and the tension I'd been holding finally let go. "I remember having this discussion before. You're right."

"So, what will you do next?" he probed.

"There's three questions I need answered. First, where are those coordinates? Two, who put that jewelry in the safe? And three, how'd the man who stunned me know what the thief locked up in jail found out during his robbery attempt?"

"Three good questions. Promise me, while you're looking for the answers, you'll be careful. You're dealing with dangerous people," he said, leaving it at that.

"Roger that, Dad. Promise. Before I let you go, how's Mom doing?"

My mother had been diagnosed with rheumatoid arthritis when she was forty-two, and she'd had times when the joint pain made life miserable for her. She's a fighter, though. Like mother, like daughter.

"She's doing well right now. She has her days, though, as you know."

"Give her a hug and tell her I love her."

"I sure will, Ease."

"Bye, Dad."

When I'd hung up, I found myself remembering an early trip with my family to Myrtle Beach, a trip of around three hours from Columbia, but endless to a seven-year-old girl and her six-year-old brother. We were maybe a half hour out of Myrtle when my brother and I started raising hell with one another in the back seat. My mother turned around and gave us a challenge. "See how many out of state license plates you can see in the next ten minutes. Three, two, one, go!"

My brother and I had rushed to accept the challenge.

With the ten minutes up, my mother asked me how many I'd seen. "Five," I told her.

"Ha ha!" gloated my younger brother. "I saw seven!"

Mom, always the fair arbiter, asked me what states they were.

"Florida, number TR3-1266, North Carolina number CNS-1422, Georgia number PAN2454, Washington, DC number SA8423, and another North Carolina one, number GAP-3394," I recited. "There were three others, but I couldn't read all their numbers before they moved away."

Mom stared at Dad a moment, then turned her attention to my brother. "What were your seven states, Junior?" she asked, expectant.

Two North Carolina, a Florida, a Tennessee, a Virginia, maybe two Alabama, I think," he said, hesitating.

"You don't remember any of the numbers?"

"No. I didn't think I needed to," Junior replied, a small whine coming through in his voice.

"That's okay, Junior. You did well." Then she turned her attention back to me. "Can you tell me those numbers again, Ease?" she prompted.

"Uh huh." I closed my eyes, saw the plates in my mind, recited their numbers again.

When I'd finished, Mom said, "You both did a fantastic job. I'm impressed!" Then she reached her arm to rest on Dad's shoulder and whispered something to him. I couldn't hear what. I did hear what Dad said back to her, though. It was a new word for me: *unfuckinbelievable.*

Not long after that, Mom took me to see a doctor. He was all dressed up with a fancy jacket and a bow tie, and his hair was slicked down on his head. I could see places where his scalp showed through.

He had me sit in a chair facing him, and then he showed me different cards with numbers and letters on them. He asked me to try and remember what I saw. He started out showing me three cards, then four, then five, then asked me to repeat what I'd seen. I did so.

His eyebrows raised in surprise.

He showed me another five cards and asked me to say what was on them. I started by repeating the first three cards, then recited the next five ones.

Once again, his eyebrows arched up. He considered me a moment, and then got out another bunch of cards which had a lot more printed on them. He selected ten cards, showed them to me one at a time, and told me to repeat what I'd seen. I started with the first fifteen he'd shown me and ended with the last ten.

This time his eyebrows danced up and down, which made his bow tie go up and down, too. "You wait right here, Esther." He got up and left his office.

A moment later, he came back into the room, this time he had Mom with him. He had her sit in another chair and handed her the 25 cards arranged in the order he'd shown them to me.

"You look at the cards, Mrs. Kelly, while Esther tries to remember."

Then he turned his attention back to me. "Now, Esther, start at the beginning and tell me again what you saw on the cards."

I did so, taking my time so I wouldn't make a mistake. I spoke clearly, so Mom could hear me, too. As I went through the cards in my head, Mom followed along with the cards in her hand. When I finished the last one, I looked at Mom.

She was staring at me, her mouth hanging open.

"What's wrong, Mom?" I asked her, thinking I'd done something bad.

"Nothing's wrong, EZ. You did great. I'm surprised by you, is all." She gave me one of her warm smiles, reassuring me. She made eye contact with the doctor and asked, "What does this mean?"

He sat back in his chair, his fingers steepled in front of his face and rested his thumbs on his chin. "I have a new word for you, Mrs. Kelly. The word is eidetic."

"Eidetic?" Mom repeated.

"Yes. Eidetic. It describes a person with a complete photographic memory. Anything eidetic people see is filed away in their memory banks to be brought out whenever or wherever needed. It is both a blessing and a curse. A blessing because they can recall easily what they have seen, and use that ability for great benefit. A curse because the memories are all there, lurking in the recesses of their brains forever, perhaps bringing pain and suffering when they reemerge. For you and me and most people, some memories are best forgotten. An eidetic doesn't have that luxury, although they can teach themselves to build clever walls in their heads to seal away the really bad ones."

"I don't know whether to be happy for her, or to be sad," Mom said, a wistful expression on her gentle face.

"Exactly. Esther has been given a great gift. How she chooses to use it will determine whether it will be a blessing or a curse for her," he explained.

"How can I guide her in the direction of the blessing side?" she asked.

"Sadly, nothing that I know of, Mrs. Kelly. She will need to learn how best to handle her gift in a way that works best for her."

As it turned out, the doctor knew what he was talking about. It has been up to me to learn how to deal with my gift. After much trial and error, I've learned how to build my mind walls to seal off the memories I never want to hear from again. Most of the time it works. Sometimes, though, in spite of my determination, some of the bad ones reach out and bite me when I'm least expecting it. It's a reminder to me that the struggle will always be there, and the only way forward is to continue making improvements. Like now, I had to put those memories of the creep assaulting me in the far recesses of my mind, but I won't forget his face until I find him and even the score. Sometimes the curse is worse than the blessing. Like now.

Chapter Four

Day Four

When I showed up for my shift the next night, chaos and confusion reigned. Two police cruisers, light bars flashing, dominated the entrance to the Adriatic Hotel. Inside, four officers had taken charge and were busy interviewing the staff.

As I walked in, one of the officers spotted me and rushed to intercept me. "Sorry, Miss. You can't come in here," he announced, his arm outstretched towards me.

"I work here," I said in a calm voice. "My shift starts at eleven. What's going on?"

One of the on-duty desk clerks overheard me. "It's true, officer. She's here to relieve us," she said, making eye contact with me as she spoke.

"All right. Stay, but keep out of the way of the search," he warned me.

"Okay, sure. What did they get away with?"

"How'd you know it was a robbery, and with more than one suspect involved?" the officer asked, suddenly more interested in me.

I cocked my head at him. "There have been three attempted

robberies here in the last three nights while I've been on my shift, and now I come to work to find this," I replied, sweeping my arm over the scene.

"What're you talking about?" the officer shot back, a puzzled look on his face.

It struck me as strange that this officer didn't know about the earlier robbery attempts. Or maybe he did, but was playing it cool, watching to see my reaction.

I considered the possibilities and decided to give him a pass. "Call Lieutenant Lopez or Officer Andrew Jackson. They'll fill you in." I watched him radio in and speak briefly to whoever had answered. Probably Lopez. Then he strode over to me.

"Lieutenant Lopez is on his way. He says for you to stay put," the officer instructed me.

"I have no pressing commitments," I told him.

Lopez was true to his word. He marched into the busy lobby less than ten minutes later. He first spoke to the officer in charge. Then he approached me.

"My, my, Miss Kelly. Trouble seems to follow you," he began, a faint smile tracing its way over his features. He reached a hand out to me in greeting.

"I had nothing to do with this," I said, ignoring his extended hand while sweeping an arm over the activity around me. "I walked in on this when I came to work."

"Makes me wonder how a sweet young lady like you could get mixed up in something like this," he said, making a sweeping gesture of his own.

"Am I a suspect?" I asked, arching my eyebrows.

"Let's just say it's one hell of a coincidence," Lopez said, his eyes boring into mine.

"Well, good luck with that," I shot back, returning his stare.

"If we need to, we know where to find you."

"I'm not going anywhere," I replied evenly, "in spite of your earlier suggestions otherwise."

"Good. Now if you'll excuse me, I need to get some answers." With that, he turned and approached the group of officers at the reception counter.

I watched him move from officer to officer, gathering information. I spotted Marie Arborio, one of the desk clerks I'd come to replace, standing by herself near the tour desk. I wandered over to her.

"Hey, Ricecakes, how's it going?" Marie had picked up the nickname as a child when a curious classmate made the discovery that Arborio was an Italian rice used to make risotto. It had followed her into her adult life.

"Hey, EZ. Welcome to bedlam central." A big smile filled her full, chubby face.

"You got that right," I said. "I get three attempted robberies in a row, and now you get one. Somebody really wanted something bad, I'm guessing."

"Uh huh. Only this time it was two guys with guns. Even *you* would've had trouble with that."

I smiled and nodded in agreement, though inwardly I went over the many times my dad and I had trained together to take down multiple assailants.

"What did they get?" I asked, already knowing.

"That's the strange thing. The only thing they took was a bag of men's jewelry. They dumped it out on the counter in front of me and had a good look at it before stuffing it all back in the bag and taking off with it."

"Did anything stand out at you when they dumped it out?"

"You mean, like unusual? Yeah, there was a giant-sized gold ID bracelet, looked like it was made for Goliath. The rest of the stuff looked ordinary next to it," Ricecakes added.

"Maybe Goliath is behind all this," I said, grinning.

"Could be," Ricecakes allowed. "Hey, wouldn't that be something? I think there might be a story there," she said, looking thoughtful.

"You should get on it. I'll come to your book signing," I said, playing along.

"You'd better, because I'll write the dedication to you for giving me the idea."

"Anything about the two guys stand out?" I asked her, getting serious again.

"Yeah. One of them was wearing the ugliest pair of sneakers I've ever seen. Neon green and gold. Couldn't miss them. I mentioned it to the police."

Remembering my own run-in with them, I silently agreed.

At that moment Lieutenant Lopez's commanding voice cut through the general hubbub in the lobby. "Thanks, everyone, for your time and patience. We're done here. If anyone thinks of anything else that might help us in our investigation, please call me any time. Name's Lieutenant Marco Lopez of the South Miami Police Department. I've left a bunch of my cards on the counter for you. Should be enough to go around."

With a sweep of his arm, he waved the officers to follow him.

Once a semblance of calm had taken over, Ricecakes and I walked over to the desk enclosure and joined Anna Parsons, the other day clerk. After Anna and Ricecakes had vented their feelings over what had happened, they debriefed me on the day's activities, all of which was dwarfed by the robbery.

Anna and Ricecakes grabbed their personal belongings, said they hoped I'd have a quiet evening, and made their way to their parked cars. I stood behind the counter, watching them leave.

A glance at the clock told me it was nearly midnight. Quiet hours fast approached. I waited another half hour, making sure the cops didn't reappear to check something else, and made sure no hotel customers had been hanging out in the street, waiting for the lobby to clear out.

When it became obvious I had the lobby to myself, I moved to the tour desk and opened the drawer for the three-pack of flash drives. My mouth dropped open as I set it on the desk.

One of the flash drives was missing. I saw only two in the pack.

I'd tucked the third flash drive, the one I'd copied the files on, back into the package. At the time, it seemed like the safest place to hide it. It hadn't crossed my mind that the tour desk operator might use one.

With a sinking feeling, I fired up the computer. I stuck the first of the two flash drives into a USB port and checked the screen. "Contents: empty."

I pulled it out and inserted the remaining one.

"Yes!" I almost shouted, then searched around me for anyone who might've heard my outburst.

No one.

Relieved, I turned back to the file I'd downloaded. It was all there. All three lines of it.

I removed the flash drive and tucked it into my pantsuit pocket. I figured it was safe there. The thieves now had the original, so why would they bother to come back for a duplicate?

After making sure the file hadn't copied onto the computer's hard drive, I turned it off and put the remaining flash drive in the desk drawer.

I returned to the reception counter and opened the guest file on the reception computer. I typed in the name from the card I'd seen in the jewelry bag: Enrico Rodriguez.

His name came up on the screen. *There you are, Enrico.* He'd checked in five days ago, paid for two nights. Maid service reported the room vacant when they went in the first morning. The room remained in his name in case he'd gone off and planned to return. The morning of day three, the day Señor Rodriguez planned to check out, maid service went in to find no evidence that Rodriguez had returned.

"So where'd you go, Señor Rodriguez?" A missing hotel guest, and now his bag of jewelry has gone missing. It didn't surprise me that the bag of jewelry got lost in the shuffle. It would have turned up at the end of the month when they inventoried the safe. Only now it wouldn't.

I had a thought.

I picked up one of Lieutenant Lopez's business cards and called the number to leave him a voicemail message. Surprised me when he picked up.

I got right to the point. Did the name Enrico Rodriguez mean anything to him?

Lopez paused, before he asked me where I'd come up with *that* name.

I told him I found the name on a card in the stolen jewelry bag. Didn't think it had any bearing then, but now that the bag of jewelry had been taken, I thought maybe it did.

"So, what else are you holding back from me?" he demanded.

"That's it, Lieutenant," I lied, my fingers touching the flash drive in my pocket.

"That better be the case," he warned.

"So, does it?"

"Does *it* what?"

"Does the name Enrico Rodriguez mean anything to you?"

I could hear him sigh on the other end. "Other than the fact he was found dead, shot in the head, his body dumped in a canal for the alligators to find him, no."

"Did they?"

"Did they what?"

"Did the alligators find him?"

"No. He was intact when they fished him out."

"That's good," I said. "So what do you know about him?"

"What makes you think I need to tell *you* anything about Enrico Rodriguez?"

"Hmm. Maybe what you tell me will help put some of the pieces together, and we can all come out ahead," I offered.

Silence filled my ear for a moment before Lopez broke it with, "I like you, Miss Kelly. You're smart, and you've shown that you have good combat skills. I'm going to go out on a limb and tell you what we know about Enrico Rodriguez on one condition: that you keep the information to yourself. Got it?"

"Got it, Lieutenant. And call me EZ. I like it better than Miss Kelly."

"On one condition," he said. "You call me Marco."

"That's two conditions. I don't know if I can handle all that," I fired back.

"Like I said, you're sharp."

"Thanks for the vote of confidence. Is sharp the same as smart?"

"You got to be smart to be sharp."

I sensed he'd moved me up another notch in his esteem. "I'm ready to hear about Enrico Rodriguez," I prompted.

"Here's what we know," Lopez began. "He's a Colombian national, ID found on him says he's 36. He told Passport Control he's an accountant. Passport history shows he comes to Miami about every two to three months, claims to have family here, but so far, we can't find any. Body's in the morgue, been there three days, no inquiries as to his whereabouts, nobody's missed him. Colombian authorities can't add anything. The man's an enigma."

"Thanks for sharing. Here's what I know about him. He's the hotel guest who put the bag of jewelry in the hotel safe when he checked in."

"Why didn't you tell me about this earlier?" Lopez barked, his voice raised a notch.

"I didn't think of it at the time," I said, keeping my voice calm.

"Go on."

"I checked the hotel registry, found he'd checked in for a two-night stay, but maid service found his room empty on the first morning. Since he'd paid for two nights, hotel policy kept the room unoccupied in case he came back. He didn't. That got me thinking, especially after this evening's successful robbery."

"Impressive, EZ. You're quite the budding detective," said Marco in a quieter voice.

"Aw, shucks. You're gonna make my head swell."

He ignored my response. "You got anything else?"

Decision time. I considered for a moment whether to share the flash drive data and decided to take the risk.

"There *is* something else," I said. "Can you come back down here? I've got something I think you should see."

"You're full of surprises. Why don't you come to the station? Ah, disregard that. You're at work. Okay, I'll see you in a few."

The line went dead.

I took out the paper with the dates and coordinates on it I'd hidden amongst the brochures, and typed the first set of coordinates into a search engine. When the results came back, a shiver went up my back. A map came up, with an X showing the location of the coordinates: five miles offshore, just south of Miami, no land near it. I stared at the X, my mind working on its significance.

I typed in the second set of coordinates. Same result, slightly different location, still water.

Baffled, I typed in the final set.

I gaped at the screen in disbelief, seeing it well offshore, south of the first two.

Several thoughts danced through my head. Treasure map? Someone's favorite fishing spots? Neither seemed relevant. Certainly nothing to kill over. Then again, I couldn't rule out any possibility.

Returning to the list, I noted that the entries were two days apart, first to last.

So, Señor Rodriguez, what's so valuable about this list that someone would kill you for it? I leaned back, swept a wisp of blond hair behind my ear, and guessed there was more to this than fishing or buried treasure.

I reviewed what I knew. The late Enrico Rodriguez came from Colombia, bringing a well-concealed flash drive that contained baffling information on it, information valuable enough to get him killed.

The lobby entrance door swung open at the same instant that another possibility flashed in my mind. I looked up to see Lieutenant Lopez striding in. I tucked the paper of coordinates away and stood to greet him.

"Hi, Lieutenant. Thanks for coming over."

"This better be worth the trouble," he grumbled.

I opened the door to the desk enclosure. He ducked inside, and I shut the door behind him.

"You remember your first search of the safe's contents?" I asked.

"Yeah, sure. Nothing came of it," he said with a shrug of his shoulders.

"While you did your search, I noticed a piece of jewelry that seemed out of place. It was a man's gold ID bracelet. The size of it is what caught my eye. It was huge, something made for a giant of a man. Next to the ordinary-sized rings with it, it jumped out at me."

"Go on," urged Lopez, clearly interested.

"When I got in to work, I had the opportunity to open the safe. After I put a credit card receipt in, I took out the bag of jewelry and removed the ID bracelet. I noticed a fine line around it at one end, and when I pulled, the end came away, revealing a flash drive hidden inside. I took it to the computer over there at the tour desk and downloaded the file. It made no sense to me. I copied the file onto a spare flash drive, then hid it in the desk. You still following me?"

"Yeah, I'm following," he said, clearly interested.

"Good. Shortly after that, the third thief came in, forced me to open the safe at gunpoint, then took out the jewelry bag and dumped everything on the floor. He searched through it, then said, 'Where is it?' 'Where is what?' I asked him. He didn't tell me, but I knew what he was referring to. When he looked away from me, I drove his head into the safe, knocking him out. While he lay there, I set the ID bracelet down amongst the other jewelry, then called 9-1-1. You know what happened after that."

"Go on anyways."

"After I'd given you and Andy, ah, Officer Jackson, my testimony, I headed home. But when I opened my apartment door, I got blindsided, hit with a stun gun by someone behind the door. Turns out there were two of them. Stun Gun Man searched me while I lay there, unable to move. Then he demanded to know where the bracelet was. Told him I didn't know what he was talking about. He said the man who tried to get it earlier spotted it on the floor when he came to, knew I'd put it there while he was out cold. You know what that means, don't you? He communicated with at least one of the two suspects you booked last night."

Lopez slammed his hand on the counter. "Sonofabitch!" Then he recovered. "Excuse my French, but you're right. But how?"

"I'm not sure. He went over me with a fine-toothed comb while his pal had a ringside seat. They left me on the floor with my hands zip-tied. I was able to remove the ties and run to the window in time to see them jump into a big, black sedan. Couldn't see the license plate, but when the driver tapped the brakes at the corner, I noticed the left rear brake light was out."

"Nice work. Sorry you went through that."

I shrugged it off. I didn't want to relive the experience with Lopez. Instead, I said, "Oh, yeah. The other unusual thing I picked up on was the shoes the stun gun guy was wearing. They were a garish neon green and gold, couldn't miss them if you wanted to. The day clerks noticed the same shoes earlier tonight. One of the thieves wore neon green and gold sneakers. None of it made much sense, until now. Everything is coming together. The file on the flash drive is still puzzling, though."

"Let me be the judge of that."

"Sure. Follow me, Lieutenant," I said, as I walked across the lobby.

I sat down and turned on the tour desk computer. When it booted up, I took out the flash drive and pushed it into the USB port. The file came up on the screen. I stood up so Lopez could sit down and examine it more closely.

I watched his expression as his eyes swept over the short list of dates, times, and coordinates. I saw puzzlement, not recognition.

"What do you think it means?" I asked.

"Your guess is as good as mine, EZ," he said quietly.

I leaned in closer. "Would it help you to know the coordinates are all about five miles off the coast?"

"No, that makes no sense, either," Lopez said, standing. "I'll give the flash drive to our techies and let them do their thing. Maybe they can make sense of it."

I agreed, while pulling the flash drive out and passing it to him.

As he took it, he said, "Thanks for sharing this with me. Next time you have information, don't hold it back. It could make a difference in a life or death situation," he said, his voice stern.

In that moment, he reminded me of my father. "Got it."

Lieutenant Lopez strode purposely out through the lobby entrance, leaving me alone once more.

I'd copied the info to the hard drive so he could view it easily, and now, after I sat down, I stared at the lines of dates, times, and coordinates.

The first entry screamed at me. Three days away. More precisely, three nights away. "What's going on out there that's so important it got a Colombian killed and sent four teams of robbers to a hotel safe?" I whispered.

I took in a deep breath, held it a moment, exhaled slowly. I did that four times, each time feeling the built-up tension leaving me. Relaxed, I hit DELETE and watched the file vanish from the tour desk computer. I wasn't sure if Lieutenant Lopez could figure this out. Or maybe he knew more than he was saying.

Chapter Five

Day Five

The next night turned out to be eerily quiet for a change, though I caught myself glancing up every time I heard a stray sound. The one thing I had in spades: plenty of time to ponder what could be happening in the middle of the night, five miles offshore, every two nights, over the course of the next six days. Had to be something significant to get a man killed and six others locked up.

I did a map search, starting at Miami Beach and moving east, trying to find an island or atoll or reef to explain the locations of the coordinates. There was nothing between Florida and Bimini, and Bimini was fifty miles out.

I considered what could be happening at coordinates well off the coast. My first thought: two or more boats meeting. Okay, but why? How about one boat transferring something to a second boat? Something illicit that required secrecy? The obvious answer: drugs. It fit. Enrico Rodriguez came from Colombia, and Colombia grew one hell of a lot of coca, which got refined into cocaine and crack in well-camouflaged jungle labs. Is that the only possibility? No. I've been taught by an ex-military dad to consider all possibilities, regardless of how remote they might seem at the time.

What about illegals? Bring them here by boat from Central or South America, then transfer them to a US-registered boat for the short trip to the mainland. Seems like a lot of effort to get a few illegals into the country. Hell, they can stroll across the Mexican border any time they want, no problem.

A shiver went up my spine, the second one in as many days. What if the cargo was terrorists instead of illegals, smuggled into the US in the dead of night? Two or more at a time to reduce the chances of detection, times three different meetings. That could be six or more terrorists.

I sucked in a sudden breath when the next idea hit me: what if they brought in weapons, or parts of weapons to be assembled later?

I sat back in the desk chair, my mind racing with horrible possibilities. I forced myself to calm down. Slow breath in, hold it, exhale out. Repeat.

I remembered the saying Dad passed on to me, relayed to him by a doctor friend. *If you hear hoofbeats, don't think zebras.* Doctors used it to remind themselves not to leap to a far-fetched diagnosis when a simple answer could be found.

So what conclusion made sense here? Clearly, terrorists were the zebras while drug dealers were the horses. Problem was, in this situation, zebras could be more lethal than horses.

Much more.

I glanced up at the clock, saw it was past two in the morning, decided I'd call Dad in the morning. No sense waking him up, and what for? This was probably nothing. My over-active imagination kicking in. It could wait. Sleep on it.

I sat thinking, and the zebra hoofbeats grew louder and louder in my mind.

It was all I could do to keep my hand off the phone, let Dad get his sleep. Mercifully, the night came to an end, and I drove home to my apartment. I forced myself to run through my exercise routine. That behind me, I could wait no longer. I got my phone, punched in Dad's number. He answered right off, sounding bright-eyed and bushytailed. As usual.

I went over everything I'd learned since we last spoke, ending with my discovery that all the coordinates were well off the coast of Miami.

"So what're you thinking?" he asked.

I told him.

"The zebras scare me," he said.

"Yeah. Me, too, Dad. But what's the likelihood?"

"That's not for you to decide. Or me, either, for that matter."

"Know anyone in Homeland or the FBI that I could bounce this off of?"

"I'd go FBI. Let them pass it on to Homeland, if it's warranted. And yeah, I do."

He gave me the name of an FBI agent who he knew worked out of the Miami office. He also gave me the agent's personal phone number.

"Thanks."

"You probably don't remember him, but he and I worked together in the old days."

"You're right. I don't remember him," I said.

"Call him now, EZ. This may be worth waking him up, but knowing him, I doubt he's sleeping. Oh, and when you get him, tell him Captain Kelly says 'hi'."

"Will do, Dad. You're the best."

"Well, I trained you. Now be the best."

I knew his face had a big grin on it.

After ending the call, I thought *What the hell*, and dialed the number.

"Agent Brophy!" rang in my ear on the second ring.

"Agent Brophy, this is EZ Kelly. My dad…"

"How is the old sonofabitch, 'scuse my pig Latin?" he cut in.

"He's great, sir. He told me to say 'hi' to you."

"You were too young to remember, I suppose, but he and I worked together on several, ah, occasions. He mentioned to me one time that he was teaching you some of the skills he'd picked up along the way, and then next I heard, you joined up. How'd that work out?"

I laughed. "Yes, sir. I graduated from college, then enlisted in the Army 18X enlistment program."

"Yeah, new program with a pathway to Special Forces. If you're good enough," Brophy added.

"Turns out I was. I got through infantry training and jump school, no problem, and qualified for SFAS."

"Special Forces Assessment and Selection," he said, familiar with the new pathways. "So, how'd you do in hand-to-hand and defensive training?"

I hadn't expected this phone call to be a rehash of my life. I settled in and indulged him. "I did enough to slide through, but held back on demonstrating my full abilities."

"Not a bad idea. No sense pissing off an instructor who thinks he knows it all," he joked.

"That's what I thought, too, sir."

"So you got through that, right?"

"Yes, sir. They accepted me into the SF qualification course, where I trained for over a year. That's where I showed them I could defend myself. The guys in my unit showed a lot more respect when they saw me take down the instructor."

"I'll bet they did," he replied, laughing. "What else did you learn, EZ?"

"After a year of intense instruction, I'm now fluent in Arabic."

"Mabrook!" Congratulations!

"Shoukran jazeelan." Thank you very much.

"Al'afw." You're welcome.

"You know your Arabic," I said, impressed.

"You just heard everything I remember," kidded Agent Brophy. "So then what?"

"I got an all-expenses-paid trip to Afghanistan and a position with CST."

"Cultural Support Team, right? Nice concept, makes sense. Has women talking to women, gets the other side of every story, every situation," Brophy summarized.

"Yes, sir. Went on missions with the hope I could get the women to talk when the men clammed up. It paid off most of the time."

"Did you fire your weapon?"

I knew what he meant. "Yes, sir. When things got nasty, the guys were happy to have me around."

"Bet they were," he replied. "Any trouble keeping their hormones under control?"

"They joked a lot. Sexual suggestions and the like. But none of them tried anything on me after they saw what I could do with my hands," I told him.

"I bet they didn't!" Brophy said. "So why'd you call? You looking for a job?"

"No, sir. I've gone a different direction. I'm working at becoming a travel agent." Before he could respond, I continued. "I've run into a situation here in Miami you might want to check out."

"Tell me," he said, more order than request.

I explained everything, starting with the robbery attempts, plus the attack on me in my apartment, and finishing with the information on the concealed flash drive. I gave him my thoughts on what might be happening at the rendezvous coordinates.

Brophy paused a moment. "Shit, girl, you might be on to

something," his voice was a near-whisper.

"Please don't call me girl, sir," I shot back, anger in my tone.

"Yeah, sorry about that, EZ. I still have a mental image of you in diapers," he said, chastened.

"Apology accepted, sir."

"Good. E-mail that sheet of dates and coordinates to me." He gave me an address. I recognized it as a secure server.

"Now, as to what you might have here, and this is confidential, you understand, we've had chatter suggesting an increase in terror activity. I'm going to work up a plan that'll put us in the vicinity of these meetings, check them out from a distance. I'll keep you in the loop. Meanwhile, tell your old man he's raised up a mighty fine daughter."

"I will, sir. Thank you."

He ended the call and I leaned back in the chair. I knew Agent Brophy's compliment was meant for me as well, but I'd be sure to pass it on to Dad. He deserved to hear it, considering all the sacrifices he'd made for me over the years.

I used my laptop to send the three lines of data off to Agent Brophy. When I clicked SEND, I wondered if I'd over-reacted. Remembering Brophy's comment about an increase in terror chatter, I felt right about the decision. *The ball's in his court now.*

Chapter Six

Day Six

The next night at work found me bored to tears. Staring at an empty lobby and hoping someone would come be-bopping in to break the monotony, I turned my attention to weighing the short list of possible scenarios open to me on my upcoming day off. I knew a lot of it had to do with the excitement of three robbery attempts in three nights, and then returning to my normal routine, going from three nights of adrenaline release to the monotony of registering and checking out hotel guests.

I found myself questioning the decision to learn the ropes of the travel business. This phase of it, working as a desk clerk, had me climbing the walls. I guessed there was value in it, making contact with a wide variety of people and personalities and tempers that would serve me well down the road. Tonight, though, I struggled to stay focused, keep myself wide-eyed, alert for the next arrival or departure.

I thought back on my tours in Afghanistan and my work as a CST member. Assigned to a Special Forces team, I went along on their missions to isolated villages in search of Taliban fighters and leaders. Once there, I stepped into the women's living quarters, which were always separated from the men's, and became another woman amongst women. I'd take off my helmet, set my rifle aside and shake out my hair so they could see my feminine side. Then, using my fluency in Arabic, I'd start a conversation, beginning with talk of the weather and daily activities. I'd gently steer the conversation to talk of the Taliban and their negative effect on them and their village. Sometimes, a woman would volunteer information about a person they knew to be Taliban. Other times, I'd push them to give up information about the whereabouts of Taliban fighters in their village, or nearby.

While I was busy questioning the women, my team members were busy questioning the men. My success rate always outshone theirs, because the village men held back while the women, relegated to a subordinate role by their customs, often spoke out.

Once I had the information the women gave me, I'd thank them profusely, tell them I hoped to see them again soon, and pass the information on to my team leader. Often the information enabled them to find and capture the Taliban we'd come for.

I remembered the patrols and the questioning sessions and the success. The long days of doing nothing other than going over gear, cleaning my rifle, and waiting for the next call. It occurred to me that a familiar slogan applied to both the military and civilian life: *Hurry up and wait.*

The ringing of my cell phone broke my thoughts. The clock told me it was one AM. Hoping it wasn't bad news, I answered. "This is EZ."

"Hey, Rick Brophy here."

Relieved to hear a familiar voice, not some harbinger of doom, I said, "Hello, sir. What's up?"

"I've got a fishing boat and three agents lined up for tomorrow night. It's the first date on the list you sent me."

"I remember," I confirmed.

"So, we're going out to the coordinates an hour before, then pull back a half a mile or so, and wait to see what happens. Why I'm calling, I'd like to have you join us. Adding a woman to the fishing party will make it look more normal to anyone questioning why we're out there."

"It so happens that tomorrow's my day off, so I'd love to join you." I tried to keep the surprise—the pleasure I felt at being included out of my voice—but doubt I succeeded.

"Great! Wear casual clothes, like you're out there to fish. We're heading out around ten tomorrow night. That'll give us three hours to go slow and get into position." He told me where I should meet them at the waterfront.

"Got it. See you tomorrow."

I hit END and set the phone down.

There it was again: *Hurry up and wait.*

Then, that shiver up my back returned.

Chapter Seven

Day Seven

Igot to the public dock ten minutes before ten so I could take my time approaching the boat. I wore a red and white checkered light flannel over dark blue capris, and had slipped my feet into sensible sneakers. I'd put my shoulder-length blond hair up in a ponytail and tucked it through the back of a baseball cap that bore the emblem of the Florida Marlins.

My eyes swept the long line of floats in front of me for any movement, anything out of place, as I clipped along. Old habits die hard. I caught movement—activity—around a boat ahead of me. Agent Brophy's voice reached me as he spoke to the other agents. Recognizing it, I hurried ahead.

Brophy saw me coming, and called out, "That you, EZ? Look at you, you're all grown up!" He bounded onto the dock and wrapped me in a bear hug. "Glad you made it. Come meet the crew."

Despite the poor lighting, I felt three pairs of eyes roaming over my body as I approached, a sensation I've experienced many times before. It didn't bother me. If anything, it told me I still had it. Twenty-eight and still able to pull them in.

The three agents took turns reaching out a hand and speaking their names. I shook their hands, offered up a smile and my name in return. They'd dressed to play the role of casual fishermen, with loose-fitting shirts draping down over cargo shorts, no doubt to conceal handguns or other weapons hidden in pockets and holsters.

"Climb aboard, EZ. Let's get the show on the road," said Agent Brophy, taking charge.

I hopped up onto the gunwale and dropped effortlessly to the deck. While one agent assumed the role of skipper and fired up the twin outboards, the other two scrambled to untie the deck lines and leap back on board. Agent Brophy stood next to the skipper, so I moved up alongside him to stay clear of the action.

In no time, we passed Fisher Island on our starboard side and headed out into open water. The skipper advanced the throttles and the boat surged forward.

Satisfied with their progress, Brophy turned to me. "Here's our plan. We'll get to within a half mile or so of the coordinates, and we'll kill the engines and drift. You'll have a fishing pole, we'll all have poles, but two of my guys're going to deploy a drone. It's in the cabin there," he said, pointing at the hatchway, "and fly it out over the coordinates. It's got an infrared camera mounted on it, so we can pick up anything with a heat signature." He gestured at a now-blank screen mounted above the boat's helm.

I'd used drones with IR, or infrared cameras, in Afghanistan. They'd exposed Taliban fighters lying in wait for us more than once. I had a healthy respect for their capabilities.

"Sounds like a good plan, sir," I said when he'd finished.

"Thanks. Hope it works," he said with a grim smile, his voice low.

We reached our position with an hour to spare, and the skipper cut the engines. Silence settled over us.

I looked up at the sky. The sheer number of visible stars came as a shock to me. Away from the bright lights of the city that washed out so many of them, out here with no lights to interfere, the stars won the sky. It brought back memories of nights on patrol in Afghanistan, nicknamed 'the Stan.' With only weak city lights off to the west to contend with, the stars filled the sky there, too.

I turned my attention to the boat to see two of the agents preparing the drone. Fuel got topped off, and one of them held it so the camera was aimed in my direction. I couldn't see any lights, no telltale glow, but I could see my thermal image projected on the screen.

"Everything checks out fine," one of the agents said to Agent Brophy.

"Good work," he replied. "Now everyone, grab a pole from the cabin. Let's look like fishermen."

In response, the third agent ducked into the cabin and passed fishing rods out to each of us. I took one, and saw that it had a heavy sinker attached to the end of the line. No hooks. Smart. Nobody was going to plant a hook in someone else.

I swung the line and sinker over the side and hit the bail release, allowing the sinker to carry my line out. When I thought I'd let out around fifty feet, I cranked the reel handle, and the line stopped paying out. The sinker's weight put a nice bend in my pole, making it appear realistic to the casual observer.

A glance to my right and left confirmed that Brophy and the skipper had similarly deployed their lines, leaving the two drone controllers in the center of the aft deck to tend to the drone.

I became aware of a sound. A faint murmur grew into the thrumming of an approaching boat. I stared into the darkness in the direction the sounds came from, trying to see it. I couldn't make out anything. It had doused its running lights. Then I heard the boat's engines stop, and silence returned.

"Go ahead and launch the drone," Agent Brophy ordered, his voice a loud whisper.

While one agent held the drone over his head, supporting it with his outstretched fingers, the second agent manipulated the control box, triggering the propellers to life. I watched as the drone lifted silently into the air above us, then raced off in the direction I'd last heard the approaching boat. All eyes turned to watch the screen. It glowed a dull grey, showing no images.

"How high is it?" asked Agent Brophy.

"I've got it at 300 feet, sir," the drone operator replied.

"Good," Brophy shot back.

At 300 feet, the drone could scan a fairly big chunk of ocean below it. Since they had no visual fix on the boat's exact location, it gave them a better chance of picking up a thermal image.

"Got it, sir!" the drone operator confirmed, and all eyes turned to the screen to see a ghostly image appear. The brightest image came from the boat's engines, only recently switched off. I could see the less intense signatures of two human forms standing in the cockpit.

"Hold it at 300 until we have the second boat imaged," ordered Brophy.

"Yes, sir."

After several moments of tense silence, we heard the approach of another boat. All eyes strained to make out something, anything, but once again the only thing discernible was the engine noise.

"There they are, sir," confirmed the drone operator.

The screen showed two boats in the image, the newcomer gradually closing the distance between them. I could make out six distinct human thermal images on the newcomer boat. They slowly came together, and I could see the images moving to secure lines between them.

"Drop it to 200," Brophy ordered in a harsh whisper. The operator moved the controls, dropping the drone by 100 feet. The image grew larger, showing more details.

It happened quickly. Four of the men on the newly-arrived boat climbed aboard the first boat. Then the screen showed a man passing a large container, maybe a suitcase, it was hard to tell, to the four men who'd climbed over. The lines holding the two boats together were swiftly released, and, with engines fired, the two boats separated.

With a suddenness that surprised us, the boat carrying the new passengers turned and made straight for us.

"Ditch the drone!" Brophy barked, and the controller jinked the controls to drop the drone in the ocean.

"Now everyone, let's catch a fish!" he added.

We all deployed our lines over the side and pretended to be jigging for bottom fish.

I turned and stared into the gloom, trying to make out the approaching boat which bore down on us. I had time to wonder what they might be doing when one of the agents yelled, "RPG!"

Instinct took over. I'd seen my fair share of rocket-propelled grenades while doing my time in Afghanistan and knew first-hand how deadly they could be.

Reacting on instinct, I launched myself over the side and into the water, my fishing pole making an inconsequential splash next to me.

The RPG exploded when I was a good six feet below the surface, but I could feel the shock wave through the water as the boat absorbed the detonation. I squinted upwards to see the boat's intact hull above me, and slowly rose along the side away from the attacking boat.

I broke the surface and drew in a welcome breath while I searched for signs of danger.

A machine gun began firing. I could hear the rounds chewing into our boat's superstructure.

I dove down and swam under our boat, then saw the shadowy hull of the attacking boat above me. I continued swimming, and emerged on the far side of it, away from the action. The gunfire had ceased, and a deadly calm settled over the scene.

Gambling that all eyes were directed towards my boat and away from the side I was on, I swam forward along the attacking boat, my eyes searching for the boat's registration numbers. I spied them, four feet over my head. The poor lighting made it impossible to read.

I scanned the boat's side for a handhold, something I could use to boost myself up, then spotted a porthole slightly aft of the numbers. I reached up with my left hand and gripped the indentation below the porthole, then drew myself upwards, bringing my eyes level with the registration numbers. I could just make them out. FL, Florida registration, and the four-digit number, plus the two letters at the end. I committed the sequence to memory, then lowered myself back into the water without a sound.

Gotcha, you sons of bitches!

Taking care to avoid making any noise, I dove down and swam under both boat hulls, surfacing behind Brophy's boat's bow without a ripple or a sound. I glanced up at the boat's side, half expecting to see the shadow of a man pointing a gun down at me.

Nobody was there. I breathed a sigh of relief and waited, treading water.

I heard muffled voices, then another one, distant, giving commands. After a long pause, the engines on the attacking boat revved up, and the boat sped off into the dark. The wake it made set the FBI boat to rocking gently.

I waited to be sure they weren't coming back.

Once reassured, I swam along the side and, using the portside outboard motor for a foothold, I climbed up into the boat.

The bloody scene in the cockpit threw my stomach into spasms, and I struggled to hold down the remains of my supper. My eyes swept over the devastation.

The RPG had struck the far side of the cabin, blowing most of it away. The instrument panel no longer existed. The radio, GPS, drone screen, were all gone.

Three bodies lay on the aft deck and a fourth sprawled at the cabin entrance. There was no movement. On autopilot, I moved to check each one for any sign of life, using the triage system the army taught me.

All three agents on the deck were dead, riddled with rifle fire, struck by RPG fragments. I rushed to the blood-soaked body at the cabin entrance, turned it over, felt for a pulse, or any chest wall movement.

"That you, EZ?" came a faint voice from the bloody mess. Agent Brophy clung to life.

"Yes sir, it is." Salt water dripped from my hair and clothes, splashing onto his face. He took no notice.

"Way to go, girl. Knew you were smart," Brophy murmured.

"Where do you hurt?" I rocked back on my heels, surveyed the damage he'd sustained. Though bloodied, his head appeared intact. I swept his head and body with my hands, searching for obvious deformity. It surprised me to find he had no obvious broken bones.

Then I searched for areas of active bleeding.

Ignoring the gory patches on his torso that showed no signs of continuing blood flow, I focused on a wet area on his right thigh, then gently probed his torn pants for the source. My fingers came away with fresh blood on them, confirming an active bleed.

I ripped his pants apart at the source, revealing a deep gash in the back of his right upper thigh. Gunshot wound? Grenade fragment? I couldn't tell. The sight of the wound oozing, not gushing, brought a glimmer of hope. No major arteries had been damaged. Good. Otherwise, he'd have blood coursing out of the wound with each beat of his heart.

I quickly checked him for any other active injuries, but found none. He'd apparently sustained numerous superficial injuries, likely from the exploding grenade, maybe blood spatter off the other mortally wounded agents. That may have contributed to saving his life. The gunman, seeing the bloody mess, may have thought it a waste of ammunition to inflict further damage to what appeared to be an already-dead agent.

Standing, I peered down into the cabin, searching for a first aid kit or something else to bind Brophy's wound. The water I saw there shocked me. A combination of the exploding grenade and the spray of bullets had breached the hull. Sea water seeped into the cabin. Now I had two problems. The boat was sinking, and Brophy needed his leg wound attended to.

I waded into the flooding cabin, searching for a first aid kit. I yanked open cabinet doors, spilling the contents into the rising water in my frantic search. The last cabinet yielded a first aid kit.

I rushed to Brophy's side and used the kit's compression dressing to bind his oozing thigh. Once finished, I asked, "How're you feeling, Agent?"

"Much better, since you came back," he said, his voice stronger. "And for Christ's sake, call me Rick," he added.

"Yes, sir. Rick," I replied, feeling uncomfortable using his first name.

"Sir, Rick," I continued. "We're the only survivors. The other agents are dead and the boat's sinking. We don't have much time.

I'm going to see if I can find a life raft and—"

"There's one on the foredeck," Agent Brophy cut in. "In a fiberglass container."

"I'm on it," I replied.

I leaped up and scooted along the cabin side to the foredeck. There, I spotted a plastic canister lashed in place. Feeling along the sides, I struggled in the dark to find the release. I gripped a metal strap, and located the release mechanism. I tugged on it and the canister came away.

Lifting the heavy canister above my head, I heaved it over the cabin top and into the cockpit where it landed with a dull thud and rolled to a stop against the rail. Then I crab-walked back along the cabin side to the cockpit, located the canister, and separated the halves. Inside was a rubber life raft, rolled into a tightly packed cylinder.

I found the "Pull to activate" control, yanked it, and an explosive hiss announced the raft's inflation. It spiraled and grew, filling the cockpit, straightening as it unfolded. It grew to 10 or 12 feet in length, five feet wide. Room for a crew of six, the legal limit for the boat.

A rope encircled the sides, a place where extra bodies could hang on. A canvas bag lashed to the side held a pair of collapsible oars, the only means of propulsion. No rations, no water. Good news was, no stray bullets had punched a hole in it.

Not knowing how long we'd be drifting before we got picked up, I thought to retrieve the six-pack of water I'd spotted in the cabin. Then I dragged the raft over the side into the water and secured it with a deck line.

Agent Brophy went in first. I helped him onto his feet, then supported him while he eased himself over the rail and down into the bobbing raft. I could tell he was in a lot of pain by the way he gasped, sucking in air with each movement.

With "No man left behind" firmly planted in my psyche from my army days, I searched each of the inert bodies for anything I could use. After, I dragged them over to the rail and hastily lowered them into the raft below, being careful not to drop them onto Rick.

I'd found two Glock 9mm handguns and secured them in my waistband in the small of my back. I also found a tactical light and pocketed it. I'd hoped to find a cell phone, but had no such luck.

I noted that sea water had begun flowing over the rear deck and the engines were beginning to submerge, the bow pointing higher and higher in the night sky. Time to get out of Dodge.

I freed the deck line, swung myself over the rail and dropped carefully into the raft. I gave a strong shove against the boat's side, sending the raft lumbering out and away. With the space widening between us, I pulled the oar sections from the bag and assembled them, clicking the three sections of each oar together, one by one.

I pushed each shaft through the rubber oarlock on each side, and sitting on the inflated thwart that stretched from side to side, I began rowing away from the stricken boat. When it made its final dive to the bottom of the ocean it would create a vortex capable of capsizing us, maybe even drawing us down with it. Not a pleasant prospect.

Reassured that I had established enough distance between the two crafts, I rested, watching the sinking boat's death throes. Its bow pointed higher and higher, and then, with a final surging splash, the entire boat slid sternward and disappeared. A strong wave created by the sinking boat rolled at us, but the raft floated up with it and dropped down the other side.

I felt alone, despite my four companions. Three were inert, and the fourth had serious injuries. For all the world, I was on my own.

Glancing around, I could see a faint glow in the sky behind me. "That has to be Miami, and west," I guessed. It provided a landmark, a focal point.

I scanned the eastern sky for a bright star I could use as guidance. By keeping the chosen star in the same place, I'd be able to maintain my heading towards Miami's beckoning glow without having to turn around and look from time to time.

Knowing I had a long journey ahead of me, I set a pace that I could maintain without having to take a break. Settling into a slow but steady rhythm, I moved the raft along. Agent Brophy, who was stretched out at my feet in the rear section of the raft, lay still. From time to time, I asked him how he was doing.

"Doin' great!" was his stock reply. The strength of his voice told me he continued to hold his own.

I lost all sense of time. My cell phone, my source of a clock, was back in the glove box of my VW. Now my only reference to time became the stars overhead and any change in the eastern horizon.

Each time I checked behind me to confirm that I continued moving in a line for Miami, I searched for some indication that I'd closed the gap. The brightness in the western sky never seemed to change. It was as if I rowed against a current equal to my forward momentum, keeping me and the raft fixed in the same position in the ocean.

My increasing thirst got the better of me, and I paused to get a bottle of water. I offered one to Brophy. He took it from me and drank greedily, finishing with a satisfied sigh. "That tasted fantastic, EZ. Thanks."

I hoped it wouldn't be coming back up.

Time passed, and the night stretched on. The rendezvous with the two other boats had been at one O'clock. I figured it had to be close to two when I'd launched the raft and the boat sank, so I reasoned that dawn had to be coming soon. As I rowed, I stared at the eastern horizon, willing it to show me some light, some change, some hope.

Chapter Eight

Day Eight

The first sign of the approaching dawn came with a dimming of the stars I'd been using for reference. At the same time, the eastern sky began to change. I could make out the line where sky and water meet. It was a relief to me, but at the same time, brought concern. I'd lost my focal point to steer by. The stars were fading, and the eastern horizon stretched farther and farther with each passing moment.

I turned around to get a bearing on Miami's glow, and that, too, had faded. The western horizon, like the eastern one, looked the same. I stopped rowing, all my references gone.

"What's wrong?" Brophy asked, worry showing in his weak voice.

"Nothing," I said, struggling to keep my voice calm. "I'm taking a break is all, Rick."

"That's good, EZ. You deserve it."

In addition to the lack of reference, I began thinking I was hearing things. A plane, maybe. It continued to grow in intensity until I had no doubt. It had to be a boat. Searching for us?

Or maybe they were out to make sure there were no survivors. Not a good thought.

As the darkness faded and light became more dominant, I scanned the ocean in the direction the engine sounds were coming from.

First there was nothing.

Eventually, I could make out the vague silhouette of a boat. White hull, moving slowly in a zig-zag pattern. When I realized what it was, I gave out a whoop of relief and leapt to my feet, waving the two paddles back and forth overhead, trying to draw the boat crew's attention. I spotted the red markings identifying it as a Coast Guard cutter.

"What is it, EZ?" came Brophy's faint voice.

"It's a Coast Guard cutter, sir. We have to hope they see us," I said. I continued holding the paddles aloft, swinging the blades back and forth in their direction.

"You want a job?" asked Brophy, his voice louder, stronger.

As I watched, the Coast Guard cutter made a course change and headed in our direction. "I think they see us!" I said to Brophy, at the same time ignoring his question.

They had, indeed.

They closed the gap between us in no time and hove to alongside the raft. Practiced hands secured the raft to the cutter's side, then a gangway was lowered in place. A US Coast Guardsman climbed down, surveying the situation as he did so.

"How many survivors?" he asked.

"Me and one other," I said, gesturing to Agent Brophy, "and he's got serious injuries. The other three, I didn't want to leave them behind." The guardsman nodded, understanding.

The crew swung a Stokes litter attached to a small winch over the side and lowered it to the raft. The guardsman on the gangway guided it so it rested next to Brophy, then he stepped aboard the raft. Together, we helped move Brophy into the litter. Once he'd been secured, the guardsman gave a wave and the litter was hauled up. It disappeared from view over the rail.

A short time later they lowered it again, and the same sequence was followed to haul the bodies of the three dead agents aboard, one at a time.

"You want to go up in the Stokes?" he asked me when it was my turn.

"No, thanks. I'll take the stairs," I said, smiling at him.

He helped me to the gangway, then noticed the two handguns sticking out of my capris, behind my back.

"Gun!" he yelled, then threw an arm around my neck, intent upon restraining me.

I reacted on instinct.

I grabbed his encircling hand and wrenched it up and away, then spun him around. I was milliseconds away from heaving him over the side when the voices from above cut through to me.

"Freeze!" came two shouts simultaneously.

I looked up to see two guardsmen with rifles aimed directly at me. I slowly raised my hands. "Sorry," I said to the guardsman in the raft with me. "That was a knee-jerk reaction. Take the guns. They belonged to the agents you hauled aboard."

"She's okay!" shouted an officer from above. "Agent Brophy's vouched for her."

The rifles were quickly lowered as I drew a sigh of relief. The guardsman in the raft, recovered, cautiously removed the two Glocks from the small of my back, then steered me towards the gangway, his hand guiding me.

I climbed the gangway and stepped onto the deck where the three dead agents, now in body bags, were lying. I saw no sign of Brophy.

"Where's Agent Brophy?" I asked of nobody in particular.

The officer who'd called off the rifles stepped forward. "He's in sick bay. Our physician assistant is tending to his injuries."

"Thank you," I said, relieved.

"I'm Captain Blankenship," he announced, extending his hand.

I shook his hand while taking in his short-cropped salt and pepper hair and his broad, weathered face. "Esther Zane Kelly, sir," I replied. "Call me EZ. Everyone does."

"Pleasure. Agent Brophy's already told us we can trust you. Now, if you'll follow me, Miss Kelly, I'd like to get you checked out. Then I'll need a statement from you."

"Sure. I'm fine, really. A glass of water would hit the spot, though."

I realized it had been some time since I'd sucked down that bottle of water in the raft, and my throat was dry. I was most likely dehydrated, too, from my long exposure to the elements.

"I've got a pitcher in the lounge. Follow me. Then I'll escort you to sick bay so our physician assistant can check you over. We'll talk after," he said.

As I followed Captain Blankenship to the lounge, I considered how much I should tell him about the events of the night.

I drank two glasses of water, taking my time. Afterwards, I followed Captain Blankenship to sick bay. I tried to hide my surprise when he opened the door. Inside, Agent Brophy lay on a stretcher, an IV running in his arm. The physician assistant stood by him. Clearly, the PA was a woman. I'd assumed it would be a man.

She stepped forward to meet me, smiling, extending a hand in greeting. "Come in, Miss Kelly. I'm Sandy Macdonald, the PA. I've been expecting you. Agent Brophy here has told me a little about you. You've had quite the adventure."

"Yes, I guess you could say that," I said, taking her extended hand. I noticed scattered droplets of fresh blood on her white lab coat, likely picked up from her ministrations of Agent Brophy. "How's he doing?"

"He's stable. He's lost a lot of blood so I'm giving him Ringer's lactate to boost his fluid levels. He'll need surgery when we get back to Miami, but I think he'll do fine," she said. "Aside from his thigh injury, which you treated very well, by the way, he's got lots of minor shrapnel injuries to his torso. None are life-threatening."

"That's great news," I said, relieved.

"I'll see you when you're done here," Captain Blankenship broke in, then left, closing the sick bay door behind him.

"You look like you came through your ordeal unscathed," Sandy said, eyeing me. "Let's give you a once-over to make sure," she added, as she drew a curtain across Brophy's stretcher for privacy and locked the access door.

Taking her cue, I stripped off my shirt, now mostly dry, and pulled off my capris, still soggy. I stood before her in bra, panties, and sodden sneakers. Sandy stepped forward, and with practiced efficiency, used both her eyes and hands to check me for injuries. She took less than a minute, then stepped back, smiling.

"You're in great shape, Miss Kelly. The only thing I can find is some raw skin on your butt, probably from sitting in salt-soaked pants for a while."

I reached a hand behind me to explore for the raw spot, and winced slightly when I found the area Sandy had described. "You're right. That is a bit sore," I confirmed.

"I'll get you a tube of cream you can apply to help ease the discomfort. You'll be sitting comfortably in no time," she said. "Oh, and I'll get you a johnny smock and some cotton trousers to wear while we wash and dry your clothes." She opened a cabinet and took out the tube of cream she'd spoken of, then went to a second cabinet and pulled out my temporary clothes. She set everything on a chair.

"Remove the rest of your clothes. Sneakers, too," Sandy suggested. "We'll get everything washed and dried. You'll feel like a new woman after." She ducked out to give me privacy.

I shed my bra and panties, put cream on my tender butt, then sat down and pulled off my sneakers and socks. Buck naked, I pulled on the loose-fitting white trousers and johnny. The sensation of dry clothes against my skin revived me immediately.

"I'm dressed," I called out to her.

Sandy came back into sick bay and got me a pair of disposable slippers for my feet.

"Can I have a word with Agent Brophy? Alone?"

"'Course you can!" came Brophy's voice from behind the curtain. Sandy smiled and pulled the privacy curtain away so I could approach the head of his stretcher.

I stepped up to Brophy's stretcher and placed a hand on his arm. "How're you feeling, s-Rick?" I asked, catching myself before 'sir' got completely out.

"S'Rick, am I? Guess that's a step up from 'sir'," he said, a faint smile playing on his lips.

I watched as Sandy moved to the far side of the room, giving me as much privacy as the small area could provide. I leaned over the side of Brophy's gurney, and, in a low voice, asked him how much I should tell Captain Blankenship.

"I told him we were on a search mission and got attacked by an unknown craft. That's all he needs to know," breathed Brophy.

"Got it," I whispered. "See you soon."

"EZ. Your old man is one lucky dad."

I knew what he meant. "Thanks, Rick." I smiled inwardly, realizing I'd used his name and it had felt fine.

Captain Blankenship had coffee and biscuits waiting for me when I reached the lounge. I eyed the simple food, realizing how hungry I was.

"Eat, then we'll talk," Blankenship suggested.

I didn't need to be told twice. I ate two biscuits, washing them down with the strong black coffee. I left one of the biscuits on the plate. My mother always told me not to take the last of anything. If you ate it all, it was a message to the host or hostess that they didn't provide enough. I doubted Captain Blankenship had made the biscuits, but who knew? Anyway, old habits die hard.

I brushed the crumbs from my mouth. "I guess you want to hear my side of the story, Captain?"

"Yes, please. We pick up someone drifting in a raft, we like to know what got you there," Blankenship replied, a serious expression on his weathered face.

"Okay," I said, gathering my thoughts. "I joined up with Agent Brophy and his men to search an area he suspected might be a drug drop. We headed out last night at around ten, and got to the suspected transfer point at around midnight. We heard a boat approaching, and then a second boat approaching, too. We moved a little closer to try and see what was going on, and one of the boats came flying at us. They must have had some really good radar or something, because we weren't displaying any lights."

"Go on," he said.

"Anyway, they closed on us fast and a spotlight came on, lighting us up. Then one of the agents yelled 'RPG!' and I reacted instantly by diving over the side of our craft into the water. The RPG exploded in our boat, and I swam under it and came up on the far side of the attacking boat. When I surfaced, I could hear automatic rifle fire. Then everything went quiet." I paused to take a sip of coffee.

"Someone on the attacking boat yelled 'Let's get out of here!' and I dove back down and swam under both boats again and came up on the far side of our boat. The attacking boat took off. I climbed back on board to find three dead agents and a badly injured Agent Brophy. I treated Agent Brophy's wounds as best I could, then got the life raft deployed. The automatic rifle fire and the RPG had punched holes in the hull and the boat was sinking, so I had to work fast. I helped get Agent Brophy in the raft, and I dropped the three dead agents down into it, then climbed down myself. I hadn't rowed more than fifty feet away from the boat when it sank."

I took a deep breath, and when I exhaled I felt the tension I'd carried through the night slipping away. I was safe.

"I could see the lights of Miami in the night sky. I locked onto several stars to the east so I could keep a steady course towards the lights. I rowed through the night, or what was left of it, and when the sun came up, there you were."

"That's some story," Blankenship said. "You know, if you hadn't held your oars up and waved them, we might have missed you. Our radar picked up the blips your aluminum oars made."

"Thank God for that," I breathed, remembering my frantic waving of the oars.

"A couple more questions, and then we're done. First, how did you, a civilian, get included in an FBI search mission?"

There it was, the big question. I considered how much I should divulge, decided on caution.

"Agent Brophy and my dad are old friends from their days in Special Forces, and he knew I had an interest in maybe joining the FBI, so he invited me to come along. He's known me since I was waddling around in diapers," I added, smiling.

"Okay. Second question, and I'll make it the last. Where'd you learn to react to an incoming RPG, swim under two boats, then swim back under two boats, all without any injuries?"

I laughed. "I spent time in Afghanistan in Special Forces myself," I said without pause, then shrugged. "Oh, and my dad taught me a thing or two about self-defense."

"That explains how quickly you broke my man's choke hold on you," said Blankenship, clearly impressed.

"Afraid I acted without thinking," I admitted.

"A different situation, it could have saved your life," said Blankenship. "Hey, thanks for giving me the details. Sorry you had to go through all that, Miss Kelly. We're heading to Miami full speed, and an ambulance will meet us at the dock to take Agent Brophy to the hospital. Do you need us to arrange transportation for you?"

"No. I left my car not far from there, so I'll be okay," I said. "But thanks for the offer."

"No problem. If you'll head back down to sick bay, I'm guessing Ensign Macdonald will have your clothes ready for you."

"Will do. And, Captain, thanks for breakfast. It hit the spot."

"You're more than welcome," he said, smiling warmly.

***

I knocked lightly on the sick bay door.

After a brief pause, Sandy opened it and rewarded me with a broad grin. "Your timing is perfect. Your clothes came back moments ago. Come on in and change.". She swung the curtain across Brophy's stretcher. "Your car keys got cleaned, too," she added, holding them up for me to see.

"Welcome back, EZ. Miss Macdonald's taking great care of me," he said, his voice stronger.

"Glad to hear you're feeling better," I shot back. I quickly stripped off the loose pants and johnny, replacing them with my own clean, dry clothes, patting my pocket to feel my key ring. It felt good to be reunited with old acquaintances. I pulled the curtain back from Brophy's stretcher.

"You look as good as you did when we set out," Brophy commented, eyeing me.

"Thanks. I could use a shower and a shampoo, but that can wait.

I'll see you to the hospital first," I said. I bent down close to him and whispered, "I got the boat's registration number."

"Holy shit! How'd you do that?" he whispered, clearly surprised. I told him.

"God damn, girl! You're good! Have I told you you're good?" he asked.

"Have I asked you not to call me *girl*?" I shot back.

"Yeah, yeah, okay. Hey, call the FBI office when you get back, ask for Special Agent Howard Yukon, like Sergeant Preston of the Yukon. Give him the registration number. He'll find that boat. And don't bother coming to the hospital with me. I'm guessing they'll keep me plenty busy for a time. Come by later if you want, okay?"

"Will do. Sounds like a plan."

***

The transfer from the Coast Guard cutter to the ambulance went smoothly. I told Brophy I'd call the hospital and drop by to see him when he had some free time. He said that sounded good.

When I glanced around and got my bearings, I realized my car was parked a long hike from the Coast Guard station. I considered asking for a ride, then opted to walk, reasoning it would give me the opportunity to familiarize myself with that area of the waterfront, and maybe spot the killer boat in the process.

I set off at a brisk pace, and soon realized I'd need to walk down each dock to search for the boat. I was wide-eyed after the night's adventure, so the search walk would do me good. If I didn't find the killer boat, at least I'd have eliminated a lot of possibilities.

Each dock had numerous lines of floats leading off to docking spots, so it took some time to check each one. I saved a lot of time by skipping the docks that clearly had the luxury yachts and sailboats on them.

I got lucky on the fourth dock I checked. I spotted a boat that fit my search criteria, and sauntered slowly past it, checking the registration numbers. Bingo! There it sat. I noted the dock space number: C 48. No problem remembering that.

To make sure I wasn't being watched, I walked all the way to the end of the dock and stared out over the bay a moment. Certain that nobody took an interest in me, I reversed direction, passing the killer boat on my way back to shore.

The path to my car, without any more detours, took me ten minutes. There it sat, waiting patiently for me. I thought of the agents who wouldn't be going home. Had they car-pooled, or were there three cars parked somewhere nearby, waiting for a return that would never happen? I shook the thought from my head, unlocked the driver's side door and climbed in.

Nothing had been taken during my absence. That's one advantage of a beater car. Most thieves consider it a waste of their time to break in.

I took my cell phone out of the glove box and checked the call log. One missed call. An 800 number. Probably someone wanting to sell me a timeshare.

I located Agent Brophy's office number in the directory, hit Send, and after a brief pause, an operator answered. I asked for Special Agent Howard Yukon.

After another pause, he answered. I identified myself, told him what happened, then gave him the attacking boat's registration number and slip number. He repeated them back to me, all business, asked if my phone number was the one that came up on his caller ID. I told him it was. He thanked me, then hung up.

I keyed the VW's ignition, cranked the engine to life, and pointed the car towards my apartment where a welcome shower and some serious sleep awaited me. I wouldn't get my normal ration after pulling an all-nighter, but being alive after the night I'd put in more than made up for a little lost sleep.

As I made my way out of the parking lot, a faded blue sedan showed up in my rear view mirror. I could see two people inside. It held back far enough so I couldn't read the front plate.

With my nerves jangling, I pulled out onto the road. The faded blue sedan followed me, keeping pace.

I considered the situation. I was unarmed, and my old VW couldn't outrun a tricycle. I was a sitting duck. My best chance was to get into heavy traffic where witnesses might prevent them from attacking me. Temporarily.

When I made a hard left turn to get to a busy section of the city, I half-expected to see the sedan come rocketing alongside my VW, a gun hand extended out the window. To my surprise, the sedan hadn't followed, but kept straight when I turned.

Relief flooded through me. Maybe I was a little *too* hyper-sensitive. But then again, my alertness had saved my skin more than once.

Chapter Nine

Day Nine

The melodic ringing of my cell phone interrupted a dream of an underwater swim along a coral reef teeming with tropical fish. I swung my bare legs over the side of the bed and sat upright, nudging images of the colorful reef fish into the background. "What could be more important than my beauty rest?" I asked the obnoxious rings of my phone. My nightstand clock told me it was ten after nine in the morning. I'd slept three hours.

"This better be good news," I mumbled.

I grabbed the phone, recognized the number: Agent Brophy's office. "What the hell?" I muttered as I swept the phone to Answer.

"EZ Kelly," I said, my voice husky from sleep.

"Miss Kelly, this is Special Agent Yukon. This a good time for you?"

I wanted to say, Hell, no. You woke me out of a perfectly good dream. Instead, I bit my tongue. "Sure. What's up?"

"Agent Brophy's out of surgery and he's doing well. His doctor says he'll make a full recovery. Thought you'd want to know."

"That's great. Thanks for letting me know. Is that why you called?" I asked, thinking that if I hung up right then I might get back to sleep.

"Ah, no. Brophy and I talked over what happened in the last twenty-four hours, and he filled me in on his connection to you. He also told me about the combat skills you learned from both your dad and the army, plus your proficiency in Arabic. He also mentioned the attack on you in your apartment. Bottom line is, we could use you going forward in working this case."

"Sorry. I have a job. I work as a desk clerk at the Adriatic Hotel," I said, beginning to lose my patience.

"Yes, we're aware. I'd like to arrange for you to take a leave of absence. We'll make the arrangements so your job isn't in jeopardy, and when we're finished with the case, you can start in again as the tour desk operator. That's your next step to becoming a travel agent, right?"

I sat on the edge of my bed, stunned at what the FBI could do with the stroke of a pen.

"That's right." Thinking I'd put him on the spot, I asked, "What's my salary?"

"You'll earn the same as any of our agents. Then, if this works out, we'll give you severance pay," he explained, clearly prepared for my question.

"Severance pay? How much might that be?"

"Twenty-five thousand."

"You're kidding!" I blurted out, stunned by the number.

"We can up it, if all goes well."

He had my full attention. "What do you want me to do?" I asked.

"We ran down the registration number you gave us. It's registered to Gofish Corporation. The corporation doesn't exist. We're working on tracking down how it got registered to a dummy corporation. Meanwhile, we called the marina manager, rented a slip that's close to the suspect boat. We've bought a fishing boat to put down there. What do you know about handling a boat?"

"I've had some experience," I said, thinking about the fishing trips with my family, the ones with Paul, and the time I'd spent at the helm over the years.

"Okay, good. Here's what I want you to do. Pack up your stuff, whatever you can fit in your car. Leave the rest. We'll take care of it, and we'll store your car."

He gave me the address of a parking garage.

I knew it.

"Drive up to the second level, E Section, and park. An agent will pick you and your stuff up. Give him your old keys so we can store your car and access your apartment. He'll drop you off at your new apartment and give you the keys to both your apartment and your new car, plus he'll give you the receipt for the boat. Take a moment to put your stuff in the new apartment and look around. Then, I'd like for you to go get the boat." He gave me directions. "Pilot the boat over to the slip we reserved for it. Questions?"

"Some of these people may remember me from their visit to the Adriatic," I told him.

"Good point. What color have you always wanted your hair to be?" he asked.

"Auburn," I answered without thinking, my Irish blood goading me.

"Stop at Della's Salon on your way back. Ask for Della. She'll know what to do."

He gave me the directions.

"Look, EZ, the fact that the men on that boat attacked you, Brophy, and his men without warning, and used an RPG and automatic weapons, makes this case even stronger in favor of terrorism. Drug runners generally avoid conflict whenever possible. They deliberately attacked your boat, with the goal of killing everyone on board, plus sinking the boat and any evidence left behind."

"No question these guys are serious, sir," I replied, mulling over what he said. "I'll be careful."

"You be more than careful. Keep in close touch with me. If anything happens at your end, I want to know about it yesterday. Understand?"

"Yes, Special Agent," I replied.

The call ended with that.

I sat on my bed a moment, wondering if I was making a wise decision. Hell, I could always walk away if I have second thoughts down the road. Couldn't I?

I got dressed and grabbed a yogurt from the fridge, then meandered through the small apartment, looking for the essential items I should take. There wasn't much. A half dozen photographs of Mom, Dad, and my brother, Junior. An old one of Paul, taken at his Army Special Forces graduation, a grim smile on his face. One of me taken in Afghanistan at Christmas, holding an orphaned Afghani girl.

I packed up the photos and my meager wardrobe in a duffle, then dumped my make-up and hygiene products into a drawstring bag, grabbing my key ring on the way out. I left without looking back, not sure if I'd ever return.

***

I drove into the parking garage, followed the signs to the second floor, found E section and parked. A car door opened four spaces down from me and a man got out and looked my way. "I'm here to pick you up, Miss," he told me, his voice a loud whisper.

I climbed out of my trusty VW, grabbed my belongings, and walked the few steps to his car, a black sedan that radiated 'Government Issue.'

He held the back passenger door open while I tossed my bags in. Then I slid into the shotgun seat and he got behind the wheel. I passed him my keys and he handed me a manila envelope, blank on the outside. As I took it from him, I asked, "Do you know my name?"

"No, Ma'am, I don't. I only know where I'm taking you," he replied, staring straight ahead.

I relaxed. The less he knew about me, the less he could pass on to the wrong people.

I paid him the same compliment by not looking his way. I turned my attention to the manila envelope which contained a key ring with four keys and a remote car door opener attached, a receipt for apartment 3C, a registration for a red Fiat 500, a purchase receipt for a 26-foot fishing boat, and a prepaid cell phone with a sticky note attached. The note said, *911 rings Yukon.* All the paper work, I noted, bore my name. I shredded the sticky note.

We drove in silence until the driver pulled up in front of an upscale apartment building and stopped.

"Here we are," he said, pointing at the apartment entrance.

I got out and retrieved my belongings from the back seat.

"You want some help?" the driver asked.

"Thanks, I'm good," I replied.

He didn't wait for my thank you, so I saved it for another occasion. He pulled away, and I strode quickly to the entrance, keys in hand.

I got the right key for the entry door on the second try. Another key opened the mail box just inside. There it was: Box 3C.

Straight ahead was an elevator, and a stairway to the left of it. I took the stairs, two steps at a time, stretching my thighs. At the top, I pushed open the door to the third floor and stepped out. A tasteful sign across the hallway pointed at 3A, 3B to the right, 3C, 3D to the left.

I went left.

The door to 3C, like all the others, looked solid and well-constructed, stained a rich mahogany color. "EZ, you have arrived," I whispered to myself, then keyed the door.

It opened into a short hallway that gave way to a living room/kitchen combination to the left and a bedroom with attached bath to the right. It was tastefully furnished, from the pans, dish towels, and dishes in the kitchen, to the made-up queen bed in the bedroom.

"My taxpayers' money at work."

I deposited my duffle and drawstring bags on the bed, made sure the sink and toilet worked, then headed back out, manila envelope clutched in my hand.

I quickly located the red Fiat 500. It sat at the curb a short distance down from the apartment entrance. I pushed the remote and the car rewarded me by flashing its lights at me and unlocking the driver's door. I hurried to it and slid into the driver's seat, then pulled the door closed. The seat had been adjusted perfectly for me.

"How'd they do it?" I asked aloud, impressed. I tucked my own cell phone in the glove box, figuring the one Yukon supplied was enough.

"Next stop, Della Salon," I announced to the interior of my flashy new Fiat.

Della Salon sat between two retail shops in a strip mall. Easy access, plenty of parking.

A strikingly beautiful black woman looked my way, got quickly to her feet and stepped forward to greet me. "I'm Della," she said, extending her hand.

"You look like you're ready for a new you, honey, am I right?" she asked, a warm smile spreading across her fine features.

"Yes," I replied. "I've been dreaming of going auburn, and today's the day."

"Well, you have come to the right place, honey. My specialty is auburn!"

I guessed that her specialty would've been whatever color I'd chosen. "You must be Della," I said.

"Yes I am, and don't you worry, I'm going to take very good care of you, honey. Follow me, please." She led the way to a chair in front of a mirror, and gestured for me to have a seat.

"Now, the first thing we need to do is choose the shade of red you have in mind," she said while shuffling through a stack of cards displaying a variety of dye colors. She picked out a card, brought it to me, and asked me to select one of the darker shades of red.

"Do you have a suggestion?" I asked.

She took a moment to examine my features with a critical eye. "You have a lovely face, and I can see your skin accepts the sun's rays well. If your skin was a paler ivory, I'd suggest a lighter hue. But for you, an auburn color would do wonders for you."

"You've sold me," I said, settling into the chair. "Let's do it."

An hour later, Della held a mirror out to me. I took it and stared at the stranger looking back. "Wow! Who is that woman?" I asked, both shocked and surprised at what the new color did for my features.

"That, honey, is the new *you*! Do you like her?"

"I do," I replied, smiling.

She gave me special shampoo to keep the color from fading, and I was on my way.

My next stop was the Boat Exchange to get my new fishing boat. Conveniently located on North Biscayne Bay, the company handled every variety of boat, though fishing boats were its mainstay. I found them easily enough, parked the red Fiat in their front parking lot and took my new look into the office, receipt in hand.

"Hey, girl! What's up?" a man said to me, looking up from behind the desk.

I had a strong urge to rearrange his gleaming white teeth, or at least sweep his feet out from under him, for calling me girl. I bit my lip and committed his face to memory for a possible future revision of his features.

"I'm here to pick up my fishing boat," I said, struggling to keep the anger out of my voice. "Here's my receipt." I held it out to him.

He got up and came around the desk, reaching for the receipt. He glanced at it, then turned his attention back to me. "Hey, this is one great boat you bought. It'll get you out to the Gulf Stream and back, no problem. Follow me, honey buns."

Strike two! I fell in behind him. He'd have a heart attack if he realized how vulnerable he was at that moment. I sucked in a breath and shook off the temptation to introduce his flabby body to the floor.

He led me out back to the dock and floats, to a handsome fishing boat equipped with outriggers and downriggers tied there. Four nice deep sea rods sat in holders on the cabin top. It comforted me to know my tax dollars were once again hard at work.

"Nice boat. She's all gassed up and the key's in the ignition. Hop on, and I'll give you a quick tour." To his credit, he didn't push his luck by adding another insult.

I stepped down into the cockpit, checking the controls, the instruments. I saw a compass, a GPS unit, a depth sounder/fish finder combo, and a ship-to-shore radio. The US Coast Guard approved everything, according to a sticker on the side of the helm.

Glancing down into the cabin, there was a six-pack of new life vests and a waterproof container that held a Very pistol and four flare cartridges. Fire extinguishers were where they should be. Everything was shipshape.

I turned to the cockpit, saw it had an inboard engine accessed by a fiberglass cover.

"What's the engine?" I asked the drooling salesman.

"Don't worry your pretty little head over it. It's a good one," he replied, giving me what he must have considered his most effective lady killer smile.

I stepped over to the cover, unhooked the securing clip and heaved the fiberglass hood back, revealing a spotless Volvo Penta marine V-8 engine.

"Nice," I whispered.

At the steering console, I flipped on the bilge fan to clear out any gas fumes, heard its reassuring hum, then turned back to Romeo. "Thanks for all your help. If you don't mind casting me off, I'd appreciate it."

"I'll be happy to cast you off anytime you want, sweet lips," he replied, arching his eyebrows suggestively. "You sure you don't want me to give you a little lesson in safe boat handling first?"

I bit my lip, counted to ten and breathed deeply, holding back the strong urge to give the man swimming lessons. "No, I think I got this," I said, working to keep my voice calm. I punctuated my words by cranking over the engine, which responded promptly.

He took the hint and climbed onto the float.

He couldn't help himself, made one last try. "You sure you don't want me to give you a quickie tour? You won't regret it."

"I'll take a rain check," I said, letting him down easy.

He freed the dock lines and tossed them back aboard, then, hands on his hips, he stared at me, clearly expecting to witness a disastrous departure.

I pulled the shift lever into reverse and feathered the throttle, backing smoothly out of the slip. When I was clear, I moved the shift to forward, goosed the gas and burbled off into the afternoon sun. I resisted the temptation to look back at Romeo, maybe get a clear view of his molars as his jaw dropped. The mental image of it brought satisfaction enough.

Once away from the docks and the mandatory No Wake zone, I punched the throttle and went through a series of maneuvers, familiarizing myself with the stability and responsiveness of my new toy. It had been, what? Five or six years since I'd learned my seamanship and small boat handling with two capable and loving guides. Dad had started my education, taking our whole family to the South Carolina coast where he rented a boat not much different than this one, for family fishing trips. He'd let me take the helm, guiding me with both verbal and non-verbal instruction, until I could launch and retrieve the boat by myself.

During my first year of college, Paul and I had set off on our own adventures, renting fishing boats and going offshore to troll, trips that turned out similar to the ones Dad had taken us on, but special, because it was just Paul and me, alone together. I missed him. We didn't see each other often enough.

I came out of my daydream to realize I had reached the marina where the killer boat was tied up. I throttled back and idled my way in, searching for my rental slip.

After locating it, I reversed the boat into the assigned docking spot, then got a line around a cleat. Secured, I killed the engine and clambered to secure the other dock lines.

Satisfied that the boat wasn't going anywhere, I sat on the engine cover and had a look around. My eyes fell on the killer boat at the next dock over, maybe forty feet across the intervening water. Perfect! They'd pulled in bow first, exposing the stern to me.

I read the name, gold letters on a white transom. JANNAH. I knew what it meant. My Arabic lessons had included the word. Paradise. I also knew that one of the paths to paradise was through martyrdom. I saw nobody in or around the boat.

It occurred to me that I didn't know the name of *my* boat. The stern hadn't been visible to me when I approached and boarded her. Curious, I leaned over the transom and saw large block letters in gold. EQUALIZER. It was a perfect name.

I sat upright and considered my next move. The timetable I'd purloined told me the next rendezvous was a little more than twenty-four hours away. *Time to dial 9-1-1.* I pulled out the 'special' phone the FBI had given me from my purse.

"9-1-1. What is your emergency?"

I hesitated a moment, drumming my fingers on my knee, then said, "Special Agent Yukon, please."

"May I tell him who's calling?" the official-sounding operator asked.

"Tell him it's EZ."

"One moment, please."

Less than a moment later, Yukon picked up. "EZ? Is everything okay?"

"Yes, everything's fine, sir." I walked him through all I'd done since we'd spoken that morning, ending by telling him my boat slip couldn't have been better placed.

"That's good to hear," he said.

"Sir, are we going back out tonight, to the second rendezvous spot?"

"No. Those guys'll be on edge, looking for an excuse to blow us out of the water. We'll try another approach. What do you know about surveillance gizmos?"

"You mean like cameras and listening devices?"

"Yeah, and GPS trackers," Yukon added.

"We used them in Afghanistan when we went into a compound to search. If we didn't get what we wanted, and thought they might be hiding something, we'd plant bugs, usually listening devices, sometimes mini cams, to get more intel after we'd left. Because of the limited range of the transmitters, we'd hole up a short distance from the village and wait. Sometimes, we'd get immediate results and race into the village to catch the bad guys. Most of the time, we lay around, hoping something would happen."

"You know a lot more about the gizmos," he said, "than the average person. I'm sure you know the important thing is planting them where they get results but don't get noticed by the people being surveilled."

I jumped down from my position on the boat and sat in the captain's chair. "Yes, sir. I learned that planting them in plain sight often worked better than trying to hide them. We watched suspected Taliban ransack a room, searching for our devices, when we'd stuck them right in the open. Lots of times they never thought to look in the most obvious places," I said.

"That's smart. Now look, we don't know if they're going to use the same boat again, but if they do, we want to be ready. There's a kit of transmitters already put together in the trunk of your car, the Fiat you left at the Boat Exchange," he reminded me.

"The kit has mini cams," he went on, "sound transmitters, and a GPS tracker. The cams and transmitters are self-explanatory. The GPS tracker may help us follow the boat when it heads out to their rendezvous point. It could also help us if the boat goes to a different location to drop off passengers before it returns to the dock where you are now."

"I understand," I said.

"Good. If you can get to the boat and plant those devices without being seen, it could give us a huge advantage. Oh, one more thing. The kit includes a scanner that should pick up a signal from one of their own surveillance devices, in case they're bright enough to use them. If you get a signal telling you they've got a camera or a sound transmitter working, forget it. We'll have to think of something else, okay?"

"Got it, sir," I replied, pleased by his thoroughness.

"We've got a taxi coming to drive you back to the Boat Exchange to get your car. Head up to the shore. He should get there about the same time you do. Any questions?"

I thought a moment, but couldn't come up with anything. "No, sir."

"Take your time with this assignment, no rush. Get it right the first time."

"I will, sir."

"I'm sure you will. We have confidence in you."

"Thank you, sir," I replied, then realized I spoke into a dead line. He'd already hung up.

The clock on my new prepaid cell phone told me it was after two in the afternoon. I took the ignition key from the boat, attached it to my new key ring, and headed up the line of floats to the shore. When I got there, I saw a cab pulling up to the dock. I silently praised Yukon.

As I approached, I wondered if it was the real deal, or a dummy cab driven by an agent. I climbed in the back thinking it didn't matter.

The cab took me directly to the Boat Exchange. It took a little over twenty minutes to get there. Certainly beat walking, especially in the midday heat. The driver pulled up in the parking area, and I opened the door to step out.

"That's twenty-two dollars, miss," the driver informed me.

Maybe this is the real deal. Either that, or this guy's getting paid twice.

I took a twenty and a five from my purse and passed it forward to him. "Keep the change."

"Thank you, miss," came his automatic reply.

I got out and closed the door, and he moved off. I found my car just as Romeo opened the office door and stepped out.

"Hey, honey buns, how'd it go?" he asked. "Any problems?" He stared at me, leering, really, waiting for my confession of ineptitude.

"Everything worked out perfectly," I told him, tossing him one of my genuine smiles. "I've come back to get my car, is all."

"Oh, of course. I'm glad everything worked out."

I cut him short, saving myself from another long speech. "Do you, by any chance, sell bait?"

"Bait?"

Clearly my question caught him flat-footed, which pleased me to no end.

"Ah, no. We don't sell bait." Then he made an attempt at recovery. "I can give you directions to a bait shop nearby."

"That'd be great," I replied, still working the smile. "Can't have a fishing boat if I don't have bait."

I thanked him for the directions to the shop and parried his last attempt at building an intimate relationship with me, then I hopped in my Fiat and drove off, sticking my hand out the window for a farewell wave as I left, a last snippet of hope for him to remember me by.

Once on the road, I realized the yogurt I'd eaten that morning had long ago served its usefulness, leaving my stomach empty for quite a while. I pulled into the first fast food drive-thru I came to and ordered up the healthiest meal available that was fit for a king. Not my first choice, but beggars can't be choosers. I promised myself I'd make up for it with my next meal.

With the bag belching out its aromas steaming from the passenger seat, I headed for the bait shop Romeo had recommended.

Romeo may have failed as a lover boy, but I had to hand it to him. He knew how to give directions. To a bait shop, at least.

I parked in front and went inside. The smell of fresh bait hit me as I walked in, taking me back to the fishing trips I'd gone on with Paul.

An overweight middle-aged man lounged behind the counter. He saw me and asked if he could help me with anything, his tone friendly but neutral. A far cry from Romeo's attack mode.

"I'm looking for bait to use in the bay," I said. I figured he knew I was referring to Biscayne Bay.

"Trolling or jigging?" he asked. Trolling would be on a hook being dragged behind a boat. Jigging would be on a line to the bottom, moved up and down to attract the fish around it.

"Jigging, for now," I said, picturing myself sitting in my new boat and dropping a line over the stern.

"Will you be casting as well as jigging?" That brought an image of me casting my bait out away from my boat and then retrieving it slowly.

"Yes, no doubt," I said, realizing there was a lot about bait I didn't know.

"Is it just you fishing, or will you have company?" he inquired.

"Just me."

"Hmm. Do you have a small cooler?"

I searched my memory of all the stuff I'd seen on the boat, but no images of coolers came to mind. "No. I'll need to get one," I said.

"No problem. I can sell you one that won't break the bank. I think you'll do well with, say, a half dozen pilchard. You can cut them into chunks and bait your hook with the chunks, or you can cut them in half and set hooks in them for casting. Works good for trolling, too," he said, giving me a benevolent, fatherly smile. Worlds removed from Romeo. I liked him right off.

"I'll go get your bait and a cooler. Be right back," he added, then disappeared behind a curtained doorway.

While waiting, I had a look around his modest shop. He had everything any fisherman might need, from small to monster rods and reels, to gaffs and nets, to tackle boxes and hooks and lines. He also had a large assortment of artificial lures, some small enough for sea trout, others large enough for the big boys.

"Here we go," he announced, drawing my attention. He set a small rigid-sided Styrofoam cooler onto the counter. He opened it to show me a half dozen pilchard resting on a heap of shaved ice. "They'll stay good in there for twenty-four hours."

"That's perfect. What do I owe you?" I asked, dipping into my purse.

"You're a new customer, so everything's half price," he said, a twinkle in his eye. He told me the amount due.

I paid, thanked him, and left with my cooler and bait.

The trip to the boat landing gave me enough time to eat my meal. With my hunger sated, I parked the Fiat, got Yukon's box out of the trunk, and carried everything to the new boat.

As I strolled down the dock, I felt like I belonged here, and looked to a casual observer like a boat owner, not someone out to steal something. I swept my eyes over and around the killer boat. Still no one.

I stepped over the rail and eased myself down into the cockpit, setting the cooler and the box of surveillance gear on the engine cover. Then I hopped down into the cabin to have a look at the fishing gear the government had provided. I needed hooks, a cutting board and knife, and a landing net on the off-chance I actually caught something.

I found it all, and then some. Whoever outfitted the boat had done a thorough job, right down to a couple lightweight casting rods and reels. Plus, they had chosen a dock that didn't have a bunch of signs that restricted fishing, I noticed.

Carrying one of the rods, plus the cutting board and knife, out on the deck, I set the rod in a holder that gave me a clear view of the killer boat. Back in the cabin, I found a full pack of appropriate hooks and took one out. I remembered to grab the landing net before clambering into the cockpit.

Opening the cooler lid, I grabbed one of the dead pilchard and stretched it out on the cutting board. Thankfully, I'd left my squeamishness behind long ago. I used the filleting knife to cut the fish crosswise into six big chunks. I dropped five back into the cooler, then threaded my hook through the remaining chunk, making sure the hook circled the backbone for better stability—something Dad had taught me. I connected the hook to the steel leader at the end of the line, and I was ready to fish.

Lifting the rod from the rod holder, I hauled back and made my first cast in over five years, heaving my bait into the water between me and the killer boat. It splashed down maybe twenty feet out, then settled through the emerald water and out of sight.

I didn't know the depth of the water, so I held the line loosely, trying to feel when my bait touched bottom. When it stopped paying out, I took up the slack until my line went straight from the rod downward, indicating the bait rested just below the boat. Satisfied with my efforts, I set the rod in the rod holder.

It felt good to be fishing again.

I turned my attention to the gizmos the government had provided me. Using the sharp fillet knife, I cut the tape around the top of the box. After a reassuring look around to make sure nobody watched me, I set it on the deck at my feet and pulled the cover back. Inside were eight plain boxes, each marked with letters—three Cs, three As, a GPS, and an S. Three cams, or mini cameras, three audio or listening devices, a GPS tracker, and a signal sensor to check for any bugs planted by the bad guys.

I opened one marked C and found a tiny camera wrapped carefully in foam padding. The miniaturization of the GPS tracker amazed me. About the size of a quarter, white finish with a sticky side, it would become nearly invisible to the casual eye on a white background. The killer boat's decks were white. Nice.

The round signal sensor fit easily into the palm of my hand. Sort of like holding a ping pong ball.

I spotted a piece of cardboard under all the little boxes, stretching across the bottom of the big box. Lifting it out, I discovered a pc tablet hiding there. On it sat a sticker with a message. *Sweep left side twice.*

I turned the tablet on, and when the screen loaded, I followed the directions. A new screen appeared, showing boxes and data for each of the cams, listening devices, and the GPS tracker. Clever. I was impressed. Now, all I had to do was hide the devices on the killer boat without being seen.

I picked up my rod and retrieved my line. My bait was gone. Unattended, something, more than likely a hungry fish, had nibbled it off my hook. That gave me an idea.

I re-baited the hook, took up my pole and landing net, and headed ashore with the ball-like sensor in my hand, trying to look for all the world like a serious fisherman. Fisher *person*? Fisherwoman? No. I'd been in a man's world long enough not to need political correctness.

I reached the shore and walked the fifty feet to the dock where the killer boat sat. Without hesitation, I marched down the dock, searching for the perfect fishing spot. When I reached the killer boat nobody was nearby. The coast was clear.

With the bug sensor in my hand, I held it out from my side as I shuffled along past the killer boat. It would vibrate if a signal was detected. No vibration. Good.

As I moved past, I took in the layout of the boat and picked out several good spots to hide the mini cams and listening devices. I figured two each would do fine, based on the boat's layout. Any more than that and I'd increase the risk of being discovered. 'Less is more' came to mind.

As for where to hide the GPS tracking device, I figured the best place for it would be on the foredeck somewhere. That would be the toughest one to plant because I'd be in full view of anyone looking my way while I clambered over the foredeck and planted the device. It was also the most important device. Keeping track of the boat's whereabouts, especially if it went somewhere else to unload its cargo, could be critical. With that in mind, I decided to plant it first.

After scanning the foredeck, I spotted a logical place to stick it: on the cabin top, just ahead of the life raft. Placed there, to the casual observer, it would look like a small button, part of the structure. Or so I hoped.

With my search completed, I assumed the role of a fisherman again. I strolled past the killer boat and found an open slip, a perfect place to cast my bait. This time I did better, getting the chunk of pilchard a good fifty feet out. There was a small splash as I watched my line drop under the surface. I gave it ten, maybe fifteen seconds, then began a slow retrieve, ready to jerk the pole if I felt a strike. My bait came back untouched.

My second cast landed nearly as well, in a slightly different spot. Movement above me caught my attention. I looked up to see a pelican hovering above my bait. I'd heard stories of pelicans grabbing bait and getting hooked for their efforts. Since I didn't need that to happen, I let my bait sink to the bottom, watching the large bird all the while. When I saw he'd lost interest, I began a slow retrieve and lifted my bait from the water at dockside.

Another movement to my right caught my eye, and I turned to see two men approaching from the far end of the dock. Both eyed me with interest. They sauntered up to me, serious expressions on their faces.

"Any luck?" one asked.

"Almost caught a pelican," I said, pointing towards the bird.

He followed my gesture and saw the hovering pelican. "Damn poor eating," he said. "Fishy taste, not at all like chicken." His expression never changed. Deadpan.

"Never had the interest to try it," I fircd back, matching his serious expression.

"You on a boat here?" he asked. His implication was, 'if you're not, you're trespassing.'

"Yep. One dock over," I said, gesturing vaguely with one hand.

"Fishing better over here?" he asked.

"You know how it is. Grass is always greener. This open slip gives me room to cast out," I added with a sweep of my hand.

"You on a boat here?" I asked, mimicking his question.

It caught him by surprise. He stared at me, hesitated before he said, "We're further down the dock," with a jerk of his head. I could tell his suspicion hung on.

"Give me a shout if that pelican gets tired of hanging around," I said. "I'll be over there on my boat," I added with a jerk of my head in the general direction.

"You bet we will," he replied, still serious.

I turned away and began the slow walk back to shore, giving the killer boat one last searching glance as I passed it. The signal locator held in my hand didn't vibrate as I strolled by. All good.

When I reached shore, I turned to see the two men still watching me. I gave them a friendly, flirty wave, walked to my dock and headed to my boat. Reaching it, I scanned the opposite dock, and there they stood, still watching. They were two suspicious guys.

I tossed them another friendly wave and climbed aboard, setting my pole in the rod holder and the net next to it. I ignored their stares and went into the cabin to work on sorting through the devices I'd be planting.

The mini cams, neutral gray in color and about the size of a dried pea, maybe smaller, could be attached to a hard surface with the sticky tape backing, or to fabric with the tiny wire protrusions that extended from two sides. It had the appearance of a bug that had been dismantled, leg by leg, by a bored child, leaving one on each side. Maybe that's how it came to be called a 'bug.'

The mini microphones, a similar neutral gray, looked eerily similar, pea-sized, same attachment options.

Neither of them had on/off switches that I could see. I assumed they were on, had good, long battery lives, and that the FBI techies were watching and listening to me while I looked them over.

Thinking to check that out, I got out the tablet to bring up the monitoring screen. I saw two of the three cam boxes highlighted and two of the three mike boxes highlighted as well. One of the cam boxes showed an image of my right ankle. I glanced down, saw one of the mini cams pointed at my ankle. Good stuff. No on/off switch needed.

I scanned the surrounding area through the port window for prying eyes, saw none, then turned my attention to the GPS tracker. I took it out of the box and held it in the palm of my hand. It had the weight and size of a quarter, blank white, no giveaway markings. I set it down on a white surface and had to look twice to find it. The tablet screen for the GPS box indicated it was right there next to me.

Right as rain.

Putting aside the devices, I went topside and looked across the water at the killer boat, then along the floats beyond, trying to see my two pelican spotters. They were nowhere in sight. I hadn't heard an engine fire up, so I guessed they were lounging on their boat, maybe sucking up a brew or two. Either that, or they had a sailboat and left the area using wind power. Somehow, they didn't fit the sailor type.

My phone clock said 4:38, so I had plenty of time to kill. I took up my rod, jigged it once, then reeled in my line. Same deal. Bait gone. A clever fish had a good start on supper. Time to concentrate, maybe turn the tables on it.

I got out another chunk of pilchard and wrapped my hook around it, then cast it out towards the killer boat. As I watched the bait disappear, I counted to ten, then did a slow retrieve. I brought the bait straight down from the boat, jigged it three, four times, then reeled it in.

Pilchard still there. No marks on it. No takers.

I cast it back out, this time getting it further as my casting improved, the rust going away. I let my bait disappear, counted to fifteen for good measure, checked the sky for pelicans, saw none and began the retrieve. All the way back to the boat side, nothing.

I jigged once, twice, three times, maybe one more for good measure, but it never happened. Instead, my line jerked hard. I jerked back, and my line screamed off the reel as a fish ran with it.

"Okay!" I said to the fish. "Let's dance!"

I worked the reel, hauling in when the fish gave me slack, letting it go when it ran with it, and through it all, I worried that the smart little cuss would swim around a piling and break my line.

It didn't.

Eventually, all its heroics exhausted, it swam docilely to the side of the boat and into my outstretched landing net. I lifted it clear of the water, and came face to face with a nice Spanish mackerel. Hefting it, I guessed it'd be three pounds, maybe more.

A voice called across the water to me.

I turned my attention and saw the two men watching me. "What?" I called back.

"Looks like the fishing's good over there!" the serious-faced one shouted.

"You never know," I called back, smiling across the water at him.

I watched the men as they strolled up the dock to the shore, then I turned to tend to my mackerel. It would make a nice dinner. Some people don't like it because it's a little oily, but I enjoy the strong taste.

With the mackerel dead, I quickly filleted off the two sides and dropped them into the cooler on the shaved ice.

I searched the sky for a pelican, saw one, waved the fish carcass aloft to get its attention, and when he'd spotted me, tossed it high in the air to land far out from the boat.

He wheeled in the sky, took aim and plummeted into the water where the carcass had landed, then emerged with it hanging from his long beak.

Floating on the surface, he worked the carcass around in his mouth, and with a jerk it disappeared down his throat. Another happy pelican. No hooks to worry about.

I looked towards shore, couldn't see the two men, but decided to give it another half hour to make sure they were gone. The way they'd acted towards me raised my hackles. It was five-fifteen. Another half hour wouldn't hurt.

My plan couldn't have been simpler. At quarter to six, I'd check for people wandering about. If none, I'd get the tackle box I'd seen below, drop in the two cams and the two mikes in separate compartments, and do the same with the GPS tracker and signal sensor. I'd carry my baited rod in my right hand, the tackle box and net in my left, and head to my favorite fishing spot. The timing made all kinds of sense. At a quarter to six most people are thinking about, or working on, dinner.

The time arrived. I hopped off my boat with all my gear in hand and headed to shore. Reaching the end of the dock, I took a moment to have a good look around to make sure nobody was coming my way, no cars were pulling in. Nothing. Nobody. For now, the coast was clear.

Reassured, I went to the neighboring dock and headed down, moving quickly. I passed the killer boat and got to my favorite fishing spot, then set down my gear. I knelt to open the tackle box and take out the goodies, putting the cams and mikes in my cargo pants pockets, holding the GPS tracker and signal sensor in my closed hands.

Rock and roll!

I strolled back to the killer boat and walked slowly by. The sensor didn't vibrate. Green light, go.

With a final glance up the dock to make sure the coast was still clear, I leaped on the boat and climbed to the bow. Acting carefully and deliberately, I pulled the paper off the sticky back and placed the GPS tracker by the raft. A quick glance told me I'd chosen well; out of sight but in plain view.

I stuffed the paper into my other cargo pocket and climbed to the cockpit. The cabin was unlocked, and I moved inside without hesitation. One mike went into the curtain fabric and one cam got stuck where the wall met the ceiling. Paper went into my cargo pocket.

I got back out, shut the cabin as I'd found it, and went to work in the cockpit after taking a quick glance towards shore. Still no one.

I peeled the paper from the cam and stuck it to the right of the helm where it could show the boat operator. Then I peeled and stuck the mike on the opposite side and put the papers into my pocket. I noted the radar unit by the helm. Probably how they spotted us and blasted us. I'd remember to pass the information on to Yukon.

I searched around me to make sure I hadn't dropped anything, saw nothing. I heard a car door close on shore, decided the time had come to get the hell out of there.

After checking to make sure nobody could see me, I jumped on the dock and moved silently to my favorite fishing spot. I bent down and picked up my rod, and cast the pilchard out into the water.

The approaching footsteps caused a vibration along the dock planking that I could feel through my sneakers.

"Hey! What're you doing there?" asked one of them in a less-than-friendly voice.

I turned towards the voice, and said, "You're the second person who's asked me that today." I added a sweet, innocent smile for good measure.

Two men. Not the same ones from earlier that afternoon. The speaker stood about five ten, looked solid, had Hispanic features. Second man, also bulky and Hispanic, stood back, had his right hand tucked in his jacket pocket, a sign I had grown to dislike.

"I'll ask again. What're you doin' here?" the first one demanded.

"I'm fishing. See my fishing pole?" I said, holding it up in front of me. I assessed my options. If things got nasty, I'd drive Mr. Speaker backwards into his bodyguard, sending them both into the water. I knew it'd ruin the fishing for a spell, but the satisfaction I gained would be worth it. It'd be fun to see if they knew how to swim, faced with the necessity.

"Why're you fishin' *here*?" Mr. Speaker pursued, emphasizing his question with a sweep of the whole dock.

"My boat's moored over there," I said, with a sweep of my arm that took in the entire next dock, "and I saw this slip was open. It gives me a lot more open water to cast into. Why? Is this your slip?"

He wasn't expecting that.

"Don't get smart with me, sister!" he fired at me. "You don't belong on this dock." He gave me an icy stare. Mr. Bodyguard shifted from one foot to the other, his right hand restless in his jacket pocket.

"I didn't see any signs posted about no fishing, and the same company owns both docks, so I don't see why I can't fish off this dock, too," I patiently explained.

Did he really think I was his sister? There was absolutely no similarities in our faces.

"Don't push me, girlie!" he yelled at me.

He'll never know how close he came to going for a swim. I mustered all my willpower, and then some, to restrain myself from sending them both into the water. I gritted my teeth and held back, offered a smile instead. "Look. I don't want to cause any trouble," I conceded. "If you don't want me fishing here, I'll go somewhere else."

I reeled in my line and lifted my bait from the water, dancing it in front of Mr. Speaker's face to show him I really had been fishing. Then I picked up my tackle box and net, and turned to leave the dock.

Mr. Speaker held up his hand. "Wait a minute, sister," he ordered. "Lemme see your tackle box."

"Why? Oh, I get it. You're a fisherman, too, and you want to see what lures I use?" I said innocently.

Did he really think I looked like his sister?

"Set it down and open it," he demanded. As he spoke, Mr. Bodyguard moved forward, a solid grip on his jacket pocket's contents.

"Okay, okay. There's nothing special about my lures, though," I said as I set my tackle box down and flipped the latch to swing the lid back. "There you go. Knock yourself out," I told him, my eye on Mr. Bodyguard.

Mr. Speaker knelt down and pawed cautiously through the various fishing items in the tackle box, careful not to get a hook in a finger. Mr. Bodyguard stood guard, prepared to haul his right hand from his jacket pocket at a second's notice.

Satisfied there was nothing out of the ordinary in my tackle box, Mr. Speaker stood up. "Okay. You can go," he informed me, all business.

I knelt and closed the box, then picked up my gear. "I have to say, you've ruined my fishing excursion. Guess I won't bother coming over here again."

I stepped around the two of them, and when I'd moved a safe distance away, I turned back and said, "But I *am* going to ask the dock manager if I can fish here."

I didn't wait for an answer, and no answer came. I could feel their icy stares bouncing off the back of my red head.

When I reached my boat, I looked across to see what my two new friends were doing. They stood where I'd left them, staring over at me as I set my pole in the rod holder and climbed aboard. Now they knew I had a boat, but more importantly, they knew which boat to search. These were careful men, suspicious men, and I needed to make sure there was nothing on board to give them any reason to come after me. When I left, which I planned to do soon, I needed to take anything that could link me to the FBI, or anything that could raise suspicion. And I needed to make sure they didn't intercept me on the way to my car. Or after.

I felt confident the FBI didn't have anything on board that a search would find and raise suspicion. That meant the only items of concern were ones I had brought on board. Of those, the tablet, plus the extra cam and audio transmitters, stood out.

I glanced back at the two men. They hadn't moved. They continued staring in my direction.

Persistent sons of bitches.

Considering my options, I figured the most damning items they might find with a search were the extra mike and camera. The tablet looked innocent enough, unless they did a double swipe on the screen's left side. The signal scanner looked innocuous enough, and could go in the tackle box and maybe pass as a bobber. That left the box everything came in. The box of boxes. All those little empty boxes, with their foam-padded interiors, could raise questions.

While considering my options, I removed the two unused transmitters and casually dropped them over the side. I noted with satisfaction that they disappeared instantly.

Then I came up with a solution for the box of boxes. I picked it all up and ducked into the cabin. The loss of sunlight as the sun tracked low on the western horizon brought gloom to the cabin, but I didn't want to show a light. Working from memory, I located the stash of artificial lures, and carefully placed one in each of the eight little padded boxes. Then I set them all back into the larger box and put it on the floor.

Satisfied, I returned to the aft cockpit. I picked up my pole, took the pilchard chunk off the hook and flipped it into the water. Some fortunate little fish would have a free dinner tonight. I scooped up my net and tackle box, and put everything into the cabin. Done, I closed the access door.

A quick glance told me the men were still there, still watching. I had no doubts that my boat would be searched. These guys were serious.

I took up my new tablet and little cooler, looped my purse strap over my shoulder and headed ashore, walking as if I hadn't a care in the world. It came as no surprise to me that my two new friends had rushed to the head of my dock, and stood waiting.

"Now what?" I asked Mr. Speaker, putting an edge to my voice.

"I want to check what you got there," he replied evenly, standing his ground and pointing at my cooler.

"What are you, the fish police or something?" I asked, trying my best to look angry.

"Show her, Aldo," he barked.

That turned out to be the trigger word for Mr. Bodyguard. His right hand emerged from his jacket pocket, holding, an ugly black semi-auto pistol, which he promptly brought to bear on me.

"Okay, okay!" I said, trying to sound frightened as I calculated what it would take to remove the semi-auto from Mr. Bodyguard's hand and relocate it up his ass. It wouldn't be hard.

I handed my cooler to Mr. Speaker, who grabbed the handle and hauled it open.

When he peered inside, I said, "So, now you're going to take my dinner from me?" referring to my mackerel fillets.

Seeing the fillets and the pilchards, Mr. Speaker wrinkled his nose and handed the cooler back to me. That cued Mr. Bodyguard to pocket his gun. "Okay, girlie. Get outta here!"

That gave Mr. Speaker two strikes against him. I mentally added him to my list of assholes.

I considered a couple snappy replies, then thought better of it. No sense giving these thugs anything more to remember me by. So, saying nothing, I turned away from them and made my way up to my parked Fiat.

I turned back to see that my two new pals had headed back down the dock, showing no interest in finding out what car I drove. That made me feel better. Maybe I'd been taken off their radar.

I started the car and drove a block away, a safe distance from the docks. "What the hell," I said to the inside of the Fiat as I double-swiped the tablet.

Up came the monitoring page. I tapped the two mike boxes, thinking that, unless they turned lights on, I wouldn't see much. As it turned out, the mike boxes worked great.

I heard Mr. Speaker say to Mr. Bodyguard, "We can't be too careful."

I guessed he meant me. That told me they were on the killer boat, and that made them part of the deal. I closed the tablet down and got out my cell phone, then did a quick scan of my surroundings. All clear.

I hit 9-1-1 and the official voice answered. "Agent Yukon, please. It's EZ."

I thought he might be gone for the day but figured I'd try anyway. The phone line did a couple clicks and switches, then Yukon spoke. Connected to his cell phone, wherever he was.

"Hi, it's EZ. Calling in with an update."

"Good. Go." A man of few words.

I told him about my first encounter with Pelican Man and his buddy on the killer boat dock. Then I told him about the second encounter with two fresh faces right after I'd planted the bugs. I ended my story by explaining that I had heard the two men speaking via the mikes I'd planted.

Yukon listened without interruption, then said, "Well done, EZ."

He knew better than to call me girl. I made a mental note of it.

"Thanks, sir. I'm heading back to my new digs."

"You've earned it," he said. "I'll get a drone deployed over the boat to monitor it through the night. Tonight's the second night," he reminded me.

"Yes, sir." Then I remembered the radar unit, told him about it, said I guessed that's how they'd spotted us and blew us out of the water.

"Thanks for that. I'll tell the drone operator to keep it above the radar beam. And I'll give you updates as we get them."

"Sounds good, sir." I started to say 'good luck' and remembered Dad's take on luck. "Good hunting," I said instead.

"Hooah!" he barked.

The phone clicked off. No long good-byes.

On the way to my new apartment I stopped at a market for the basics, not knowing what my refrigerator contained. Coming out, I noticed a green sedan, its engine idling, sitting two rows over, a man behind the wheel. Couldn't tell if he had a passenger. There weren't many cars in the market parking lot at that hour, so it caught my eye.

When I pulled out, the green sedan showed up in my wake, staying back from me a conservative distance. Coincidence? Or deliberate? I considered the situation. If the bad guys had identified my car, they could drive the streets around here and eventually come across my bright red Fiat parked at the curb. So what do they gain by tailing me and running the risk of being spotted? The answer raised my level of alertness several notches. They planned to kill me, rid the planet of me on the off-chance I was up to no good. Off me on the off-chance.

With that thought for company, I drove aimlessly, turning right and left and right again, watching in my mirror to see if the green sedan kept pace. Damned if it didn't.

Okay.

I weighed my weapons. Feet, knees, fingers, hands, arms, elbows, head. All good in most encounters, but not so good against a gun. Or guns. Time to employ evasive action 101. I needed to find a place where nobody else could get hurt.

So I drove, searching for that spot.

Found it. Kept driving. Made a right. Another right. A third right, all the time seeing the green sedan on my heels, and then I arrived back at the spot I'd chosen.

I pulled sharply to the curb, bailed out, dashed for the cluttered alley I hoped would serve my purpose.

A car door slammed behind me, and I glimpsed a man racing to intercept me. Got behind the first big object I came to, a dumpster, and waited. The man overshot me in his eagerness.

I didn't overshoot him.

Came out behind him, brought my right foot upwards into his groin, felt the satisfying contact.

The man staggered, dropped his gun. I wrapped my left arm around his neck and squeezed while I shoved his head forward into the notch of my elbow with my right hand. It shut down the blood to his brain instantly. In ten seconds, he lost consciousness and sagged in my arms. In thirty seconds, he'd lost his life. Brain dead.

I allowed his body to slide to the ground, saw it was Pelican Man, the first man who didn't like me fishing on his dock. I reached down and picked up his gun. A nice Glock, 9 millimeter.

I eased back the slide, saw a round chambered, ready to fire. Full mag. I hoped I wouldn't need all that firepower.

I stuck it behind my back, pulled my shirt loose over it. Using available cover, I moved to the alley opening, peered out into the dark street. The green sedan sat there, empty. Both doors open. Bad news. I'd bagged the passenger, which meant the driver was still out there somewhere.

I searched for movement, saw nothing. Guessed the driver was hanging out nearby, waiting for his buddy to come out with a red scalp in his hand. Not happening tonight.

I had time on my side. My mackerel was on ice and my groceries would keep. I returned to my hiding spot behind the reeking dumpster, drew the Glock, hunkered down and waited. Figured curiosity would kill the cat. Curiosity, and a Glock.

I hadn't decided whether to have rice or potato with my mackerel when the driver showed up. To his credit, he came on high alert, his handgun held out in front of him as he shuffled forward, peering into the alley's gloom. Pelican Man's buddy.

As soon as he moved past my position, I stood up and closed on him, stuck the Glock under his left arm and fired, using his clothing to muffle the shot.

110

He shuddered and dropped, the bullet raising havoc with his heart, aorta. He didn't need a second shot. One and done.

To me, the sound of the gunshot rang out like a clap of sudden thunder. Certain that cars were stopping, doors were opening, people were surging out to discover the cause, I ran to the alley entrance and peered out.

Nothing. No one. I waited another minute. Still nothing.

Surprised but reassured, I dashed into the alley's gloom, dragged Pelican Man up to his partner, wiped my prints off the Glock and wrapped his right hand around the grip. Left them like that, a puzzle for the police to sort through.

Then, after a reassuring glance around, I sauntered to my Fiat and drove to my new digs. Nobody followed me there.

I closed the heavy wood door behind me, set the cooler and bag of groceries on the counter, and ducked into the bathroom for a look in the mirror. My new auburn hair still surprised me, seeing it. I had a critical look at my face, arms, and clothes, sure that I'd find blood spatter from the close-range shot I'd made.

It turned out to be lighter than I imagined. A few misty droplets on my right arm and shirt, but not much more. I shed my clothes, leaving them in a heap at my feet, and stepped into my exercise routine. No matter how tired I felt, I never skipped it. Skip one, and the next one gets easier to skip. Not a trap I planned on falling into. When I'd finished, I turned on my new shower.

While waiting for the water to get warm, I took stock of my emotions. I'd just taken two lives. They say that the first person you kill is memorable, like memories of your first lover. My first kill happened in Afghanistan in a firefight, and I didn't have time to think about what I'd done. Things got blurred, I fired my rifle and dodged around, had to use my Ka-bar. When it ended, there were six dead Taliban lying bloody on the ground. One of the Rangers on my team took a round through his head, a reminder that it could've turned out different for me.

Later, when I had time to go over what had happened and what I'd done, the whole scene seemed surreal. I never had time to feel much of anything. I lived and they died, and that was that. It felt good to be alive. Maybe tomorrow wouldn't turn out as good.

I recalled what my drill instructor had said to us during basic training. We were sitting, lounging around in a circle after a strenuous series of exercises. He'd looked us over, then said, "You're all of you killers, you know. You've been killers for a long time, you just never thought about it."

We glanced at one another, not sure what he meant.

"When you were little kids, how many of you stepped on ants or bugs?"

Everyone raised a hand.

"Killers! What's the difference between killing bugs and killing a person?"

One recruit spoke up. "Bugs don't matter, sir!"

"How do you know? You talk to the survivors? The widows you made, the brothers or sisters of the ones you killed?"

Another recruit said, "I don't talk bug, sir!" Playing the wise guy.

"Yeah, you don't, so that makes it all right, that what you're saying?"

Nobody spoke. We were all busy thinking about what the DI had just said.

The two men I killed an hour ago wanted me dead. They had no pressing reason, far as I could tell. Decided I might be a threat, so thought they'd step on me, eliminate possibilities. Hell of a thing.

So I get to run my exercise routine, step into a shower, wash it all away. They get to lie in a dark alley, the rot process already starting, wait to be discovered.

***

I found eggs and flour in the kitchen, so I did an egg and flour dip for the mackerel fillets and sautéed them in a frying pan. I found a box of green beans in the freezer and boiled them up as a side. All I needed. I sat at the kitchen table and ate, surprised at my hunger. Nothing like a little sea breeze to sharpen the appetite. Being alive helped, too.

Finished, I dumped my plate in the sink and wandered around the still-foreign apartment, taking it all in, feeling restless, out of place. I checked my phone clock, saw it was 7:30, checked the microwave clock, saw it said 7:31. Close enough.

Though it hadn't been long since my last conversation with him, I decided to call Yukon, and tell him about my alley encounter. I thought he'd likely left for the day, but figured 9-1-1 could patch me through.

"Yukon."

Right to the point.

"It's EZ. Had a detour on the way back to my apartment."

I told him what had happened, who they were.

"These guys mean business, EZ. You watch your back."

I remembered that I hadn't told him my suspicions about Miami PD. It seemed like a good time to bring it up.

I told Yukon that Lieutenant Marco Lopez had related to me that the prisoners didn't speak to one another, and none of them had made any phone calls. A couple hours later, I was ambushed in my apartment by two Hispanic creeps, one wearing ugly neon green and gold sneakers, who demanded I give over the flash drive. Someone must've told him about the ID bracelet, and if none of the prisoners were talking, maybe a cop gave out the information. Maybe even Lieutenant Lopez.

"Interesting. I'll get one of my men to do some snooping."

"Thanks." I bit off the 'sir' that tried to follow.

"You a light sleeper?" he asked.

"That I am.

"Good. May call you if the boat comes back to a different dock. Meeting time's set for one AM, so it'd be around two, I'm guessing."

"I'll be on standby."

"Good. Talk later."

He clicked off before I could respond. Not that I had much more to say.

It was barely eight o'clock, but I'd had a full day and facing an interrupted night ahead, my new bed beckoned.

After setting my cell phone on the nightstand and stripped to a t-shirt, I crawled between the sheets.

I did my Zen breathing thing and lay there waiting for calm to replace my jangled nerves. My thoughts danced over the puzzle of who told Sneaker Man about the flash drive, then settled over what still waited out there on the ocean.

Chapter Ten

Day Ten

I woke to my phone blasting out the ringtone to "Titanium".

"What?" I mumbled. It was 2:16 AM. I'd slept six hours. Knew it'd pay off later.

"It's Yukon. The boat came back to a different pier. We got a couple agents moving on them, and the drone's watching from above. You want to join the party?"

Of course I did.

"Put on the black clothes in your closet. Your password for the agents is 'Toledo'." He gave me directions to their rendezvous point. "Make sure you mute your phone."

"Roger that," I replied.

Clothes hung in the closet, just as he'd said. I took them out and laid them on the bed. I noticed the black sneakers on the closet floor, and got them out, too. I pulled on a lightweight long sleeve pullover and slipped into loose-fitting pants, not surprised that everything was a perfect fit. I picked up the sneakers, found a pair of black socks tucked inside, and slipped them on. The shoes were my size, as if I'd bought them myself. Someone went to a lot of trouble to get things right. I pulled my hair into a pony tail and grabbed my keys.

I slipped my muted phone into the side pocket of my pants, slipped my purse strap over my shoulder, and headed out the door. I carried the black balaclava I'd found in a drawer, but didn't put it on. I didn't want to startle anyone out at that hour.

Traffic was nonexistent, so the drive to the rendezvous point took me less than ten minutes. I parked at the curb, tucked my purse under the front seat, and got out. A man dressed in black stepped from the shadows, and asked, "Where are you going?"

"Toledo," I told him.

"This way," he whispered.

I followed him, moving silently in the black sneakers.

"There's the entrance they used when they got here," he whispered, indicating a doorway across the dark street. Nothing fancy, it opened into a two-story structure that could've been an apartment or a single-family residence.

"Nobody's come out," whispered a voice behind me, deeper in the shadows. Agent Two had watched while his buddy came to meet me. He'd concealed himself well. I was impressed. Felt good to be on their side.

As we stood there, the door opened and two men slipped out into the night. We ducked into the gloom, motionless, and watched. After they made a cursory search of the area, they struck out down the street. I thought I caught the flash of neon green and gold sneakers, but I couldn't swear to it.

"Stay put," Agent One told me as he and the other agent set out to follow, moving silently a safe distance behind the retreating figures.

Watching a darkened doorway in the middle of the night gets old real fast. Not being one to sit still for long, it became a test of my patience. I did deep breathing exercises, then alternated bouncing on the balls of my feet. An approaching shadow caught my attention. Quiet, on high alert, I watched and waited.

Turned out it was the two agents returning. The spokesman informed me the two men had gone to their boat and took off, presumably to the original slip where two more agents waited to confirm. He said he'd spoken to Yukon, who related that the drone had picked up audio from the bugs I'd planted. The conversation was in Arabic, and he wanted me to translate.

Glad to be relieved of staring at a doorway in pitch blackness, I finger-saluted the two agents and made my way quietly to my car. The drive to Miramar and the FBI headquarters took less than twenty minutes. I jumped on I-75 and watched my back all the way to the exit. No one followed.

I pulled into the main parking lot and grabbed a spot out of view of the street. When I pulled open the big front entry door, an agent stepped in my path. "Where are you going?" he asked.

"Toledo," I replied, wondering if the same password worked here. It did.

"Follow me," he said, then turned to lead me up a level and down a corridor to a door. He knocked.

"Enter," came Special Agent Yukon's commanding voice from within.

The agent opened the door and stepped aside so I could go inside. Then he closed the door behind me.

"EZ. Come in," said Yukon, sparing no words. I wondered if I'd ever hear him say 'EZ, go' as I took in the man whose voice I'd heard many times. He had rugged features, and the appearance of a man who didn't neglect his physical condition. A pair of reading glasses rested on the bridge of his nose, and a glossy reflection was thrown back by his balding head. I guessed his age at around 45 to 50.

I moved to his desk, and sat in the chair in front of it. A tape deck sat between us.

"Here's the transcription of the audio from the bugs you planted," he began. "Let's see how good your Arabic is." He depressed the Play switch and Arab-speaking voices spilled from the speaker. I listened carefully, trying to separate the voices, assign them to the various men talking.

"Hit the Stop button. Sir," I added, not wanting to sound bossy.

"They're talking about a plan," I said. "At first, they're saying they're on the final stretch, that the end is within their grasp. One said that the Great Satan is going to take a while to recover, maybe a very long time, maybe never. Hit Play again please."

He did. The Arabic voices rolled on, and I listened carefully.

"Stop," I said.

"One of them said that Washington would be uninhabitable when they finished their plan, and you probably heard the laughter after his remark. That was followed by much bragging that included the plan and the men who would get the honor of carrying it out. Let's listen," I prompted him.

He resumed playing the recording, and I listened carefully. I let it run to the end. Yukon switched off the machine.

"They spoke of three separate attacks. DC got the most play, but two other sites were mentioned. New York's financial district, and Miami Beach. They spoke of destroying the Great Satan's financial world and of destroying the decadence and nudity that had become the Great Satan's playground."

"Nicely done, EZ. My Arabic-speaking expert came to the same conclusions as you."

He'd surprised me, but I realized he only wanted confirmation from two sources. The FBI way.

"Thank you, sir. So what's the plan?" I looked at him expectantly.

"There's one more boatload of terrorists coming in tomorrow night, so we have to be prepared to act fast. We're assuming the suitcases contain some kind of nuclear devices. I doubt they're big enough to blow up a lot of buildings, but the radiation that they cause could make large, urban areas uninhabitable for many years to come. We have to stop the terrorists before they can detonate their devices," Yukon concluded.

"I agree."

"Here's where I see you helping us. We'll dress you up to look like a Sharia woman and send you to knock on their door. There's a mosque eight blocks from their building. We'll get you brochures for it so you can pass them out to anyone interested. If you can get inside, you can eyeball the floor plan. Maybe get a sense of where they eat, where they sleep. Maybe you can figure out where they're storing those suitcases they brought. We think they contain the devices you heard them speaking about."

"I probably should have some ID in case they search me."

"We've thought of that. It's in the works."

"Do you want me to wear a wire?" She hoped not, but she would if she had to.

"No. The last thing we need is for them to search you and find something to make them suspicious. It'd make things difficult for you," he said.

I got his point. Making things difficult could include my death. I changed the subject. "What time is the boat rendezvous tomorrow night?"

"Two AM."

"So, if they're successful, the last four terrorists could come ashore by three, three-thirty. They'll be ready to roll soon after," I concluded.

"Mmhmm. That's right. We're guessing they'll head out in three or more separate vehicles, and then keep in touch as they move out. We think they intend to detonate in the three locations simultaneously, for maximum psychological effect on the US population. We have one concern. The four terrorists planning to detonate in Miami

Beach can move out on short notice. If that group is the one coming in tomorrow night, the other two groups could move at any time."

"Even more reason to get in there and assess their readiness," I said. "Once they're out and on the road, it'll be much harder to keep track of them…or stop them."

"Exactly," he agreed.

I checked the time. 5:08. "When do you think my ID and clothes'll be ready?"

"Within the hour, maybe sooner. You hungry?"

I knew from experience I could go a long time between meals. I considered I'd be knocking on doors and passing out brochures for who knew how long? "Sure," I replied, smiling.

"Follow me. We'll get something in the cafeteria." He led the way.

The cafeteria was relatively quiet. The food selection was impressive. I could get anything from a full breakfast of pancakes, eggs, bacon, sausage, French toast, home fries, biscuits and gravy, and all the fixings. Or, I could order a steak, hamburgers, lasagna, meat loaf—the list was endless. Agents could eat based on the schedule they kept and the amount of energy they burned, or on the energy they anticipated burning.

We each picked up a tray and slid it along the food line, grabbing items as we moved along. I got more than I needed, but I couldn't resist. I reasoned that it might be my last meal for some time.

Yukon led the way to a vacant table. We set our trays down and slid in behind them. I filled my cup with coffee from the carafe on the table, then set to work on choosing what I'd try first. Yukon did likewise. We ate in silence, both comfortable with it.

I finished, slid the tray with my remnants to the side, and refilled my coffee cup. "That was delicious," I said, feeling renewed, ready for the day.

"They do well here," he commented.

We sipped our coffees until Yukon's cell rang. He picked it up, saw the caller, and answered. He listened in silence, then said, "Go ahead and text it."

He glanced at me. "The agents watching the building saw a man pull up and get out of what looked like an unmarked police car. He went into the building and stayed inside for close to fifteen minutes, then came back out and drove off. They took a photo of him when he came out. They're texting it to me."

His phone chirped and he opened the incoming text. After a quick glance, he slid it across the table to me.

I used my fingers to enlarge the image. My eyebrows arched,

recognizing the man. "No question: it's Lieutenant Lopez of the Miami Police Department."

"Interesting." He rubbed his hand down over his face.

My brain shifted into overdrive, too. I knew someone at the Miami PD had leaked the information about the ID bracelet, which set off my being tasered and searched. It looked like the informant was good old Lieutenant Lopez. I had trusted him. His association with me might've been part of a plan to mislead me. A shiver went up my back and I got the creepy feeling that I'd been set up. Taken advantage of by Lopez. I told Yukon my thoughts.

"Yeah, but why? What's in it for the lieutenant? Turning Miami Beach into a wasteland can't be a benefit to him, far as I can see."

I had to agree. I knew we were missing a piece to the puzzle.

"While you think about it, let's get you set for your campaign to bring the terrorists to the mosque," he said, his face serious.

I stood with him, grabbed my tray and followed him to the dirty dish window where we dropped them off.

A short walk later, he opened the door on a space that surprised me by its size and complexity. There were tiers of clothing everywhere, in all sizes, colors, and styles.

Ignoring it all, he led the way to a counter along the left side wall, manned by a smiling middle-aged woman who carried herself like she regularly worked out. My guess is, she did.

"Mary, this is EZ," said Yukon, introducing us with a wave of his right hand.

"That's easy for you to say," Mary replied, a twinkle in her eye.

I liked her right off.

"It's a pleasure, EZ." A warm smile danced across her strong, Indian features as her kind eyes swept over me.

"I've got some clothes for you," she continued, turning to retrieve a neat pile of Arab clothing. She held up a pair of loose-fitting pants I remembered were called *tombaan*. She displayed a light *parahaan*, an overdress that would hide my contours in its folds and a *hijab*, a combination head cover and shoulder wrap. Put all together, I'd be hiding my feminine charms, but thanks to Mary's foresight, I'd still be able to move freely, if I needed to defend myself.

"Come with me, EZ. Let's see if they fit you." She motioned for me to follow her to a changing room.

I quickly shed my old duds and shrugged into my Muslim clothes, finishing by draping the *hijab* around my head, making sure my auburn hair was covered.

"*Salaam alaikum!*" she said to me, seeing the effect of the Arab

120

clothing on me. Her use of Arabic surprised me.

"Walaikum salaam!" I replied, bringing my hands together in front of my face in a gesture of peace.

"That's perfect!" Mary said. "Now, come. A photograph for your ID."

I followed her to a camera facing a white backdrop and dutifully stood while she snapped a couple shots of my face peeking out of my new *hijab*.

"Give me a few moments, and I'll have your ID dropped off at Agent Yukon's office," she told me, ushering me back to him.

I turned to her before we left, curious about the extent of her Arabic. *"Shokran,"* I said. Thank you.

"Al'afw!" You're welcome, she promptly replied. She clearly knew her Arabic. I wondered if she was the 'Arabic expert' who'd listened to the tape before I had.

We returned to Yukon's office, took our respective seats. A small cardboard box had been set on his desk. Yukon opened it and glanced at the contents, then slid it across to me. "There's your brochures for the Friday Mosque of Miami," he explained.

I pulled out a brochure. Nothing fancy. Three colors: red, black, and white, with a stylized sketch and description of the mosque, a list of activities and a schedule of prayer meetings. I committed it all to memory in case I got challenged. My eidetic memory came in handy.

"Looks good," I said, scanning the brochure. We were interrupted by a knock at the door.

"Come in," he barked at the door. Mary stuck her head in.

"EZ's IDs," she said, then stepped forward to Yukon's desk.

I noticed a limp I hadn't seen before.

"I took the liberty of putting your old clothes in this bag." She passed it to me with a smile.

Yukon took the IDs, gave them a cursory look, then handed them over to me.

I checked each one. My new Afghan name: Aeisha Ahmadi. Nice. Close enough to my nickname to get my attention when someone spoke to me. My IDs included an Afghan passport, a visa, a Florida driver's license and a revised registration card for my Fiat. All very authentic.

When the door closed behind her, I turned to Yukon. "Where'd Mary get the limp?"

"You don't miss much, do you? She used to be a field agent, a damned good one, until she took a bullet in her knee. After, she decided an inside job made more sense, she might live longer. She does good work," he added, a sweep of his hand at my clothing, my new credentials.

"You ready to get back out there?"

He didn't add 'and earn your pay', but he didn't need to. I was ready.

When we reached the entry door, he cautioned me to be careful and go easy, his exact words. "We've got more than twenty-four hours before the last boat comes in. The main thing is to make sure the first two teams don't head out sooner," he reminded me.

"Don't worry, I'll go easy. I'll make contact, see what I can learn, avoid being threatening," I reassured him. I wrapped my new *hijab* around my head and pushed out through the door. My new clothes moved fluidly with me, covering my body but allowing my full range of motion.

As I strolled casually towards the Fiat, I had to resist the urge to do a somersault kick. This wasn't the time for that. The sun brightened the sky, the early morning when the air is cool and filled with the aromas of flowers and trees that have been charging the air all night. I drew in a deep breath, relishing it.

On the way to the surveilled building I considered my next move. It was a little after seven in the morning, and I didn't think a mosque promoter would be knocking on doors that early. I guessed most of the building's inhabitants would be sleeping after their boat trip and busy night, so I figured showing up at nine would be more productive. So, what to do for an hour and a half? The answer came in a flash. I'd go to the mosque, check it out as a Moslem woman. I made a detour to it.

I'd missed Fajr, the early morning service, and the next one, Zuhr, wouldn't be until one, but I knew worshippers came and went on their own throughout the day. I parked in the lot and found my way to the women's entrance. I removed my sneakers and tucked them into the shoe locker, washed my feet, then went inside.

The empty room felt cool in the early morning. It was a miniaturization of the one the men prayed in. The big difference was the lack of an alcove for the *imam*. Instead, there were speakers arrayed that would bring the imam's message to the women. The men got the benefit of direct contact with the imam while the women heard his words through the speakers, much less personal. It was the sharia way. Women didn't count as highly as men. Simple as that.

I had a good look around to confirm no one else was there, then moved forward to the prayer mat, a large plain rug positioned to face the east and Mecca, Mohammed's holy city. I knelt down, then rocked back on my haunches, my eyes busy examining the room in detail.

I couldn't see any cameras, but that didn't mean there weren't any, remembering how small the ones I planted had been. It gave me an idea.

To satisfy any voyeurs who might be watching me, I went through the motion of praying, my thoughts on God, not Allah. Then I retraced my steps, put my sneakers back on, and returned to my car. I took out my phone, hit 9-1-1, and got Yukon.

"I had a thought, sir. What do you think about my planting a microphone inside the building?"

"Sounds dangerous, EZ. What if they search you?"

"That won't happen, sir."

There was a pause. "It's against my better judgment, but I'll send someone down there to drop off a mini mike."

"Thanks. If I can plant it, I will," I promised.

"Don't take any unnecessary chances."

Hell, my life had been one unnecessary chance after another. I followed my dad's advice on that. "Use your head before you use your body." It had worked fine. So far.

I parked three blocks away from the building, scooped up a handful of brochures and locked the car. I walked slowly but purposefully in the direction of the mosque. A block from it, one of the agents appeared in a doorway, and motioned me towards him.

"Aiesha, right?"

"Guilty as charged," I said, smiling.

He led the way to a second floor apartment that faced the front of the suspects' building. Another agent stood back from the window, looking down. I glanced around, taking in a living room with a couch and two upholstered chairs. A small table sat between them, a lamp resting on it. A larger table and two kitchen chairs sat under the window. I saw a door that opened into a small bathroom. I turned my attention to the agents, and we exchanged introductions. Agents Will and Nick. I eyed the unobstructed view they had of the suspects' building entrance.

"Nice," I said, seeing the vantage point. "Any activity?"

"Not since the police lieutenant left," replied Will. He picked up a small box from a corner table and handed it to me. "Agent Yukon asked me to give this to you."

It looked just like the boxes I'd handled on the boat. I opened it, pulled out the foam padding, and lifted out the mini mike. I cradled it in the palm of my hand, hoped I'd get the chance to plant it inside the suspects' building.

I pulled up my overshirt and dropped it carefully into my pants pocket. "Thanks," I told Will, making eye contact. "Did you get a monitor?"

"We did. The mike's activated, so it'll pick up anything said within thirty feet of it. Maybe a little less with it in your pocket," he added.

"I'll let myself out." Time to earn my keep as a mosque promoter. The morning was slipping away. Already it was a little after nine.

To get in the swing of things, I knocked on the first door I came to. I waited, hearing locks being released. The door opened to reveal a woman's face brimming with suspicion. "Yes?" she asked, her face radiating wariness.

"*Salaam alaikum*," I responded, smiling and bowing slightly. "I have come to tell you about the Friday Mosque of Miami."

"You know what you can do with your mosque," she snarled, then slammed the door closed.

My first efforts as a mosque promoter hadn't gone well. Undaunted, I moved on to the next door. Knocked. Waited. Heard the locks clicking open.

The door opened a foot, and a wrinkled female face peered out at me. "Yes?"

"*Salaam alaikum*," I said, displaying a kind smile and bowing. "I have come to tell you about the Friday Mosque of Miami."

"I don't have time for this right now. Sorry." She closed the door, and flipped the locks back in place.

Not quite so harsh or abrupt as the first woman. I took it as progress, small as it was.

Encouraged, I moved on to the suspects' door. I knocked. Waited. The door opened and a man's head peered out at me. Seeing me in my Arab clothing, I saw him relax slightly.

"*Salaam alaikum*," I said, bowing slightly, eliminating my smile to maintain my decorum in true Muslim fashion.

"*Walaikum salaam*," he returned, nodding ever so slightly.

Ah. Better.

"I have come to tell you about the Friday Mosque of Miami," I continued, holding up my handful of brochures as evidence.

He hesitated a moment, looking me over. Then he stepped back, opening the door wide. "Enter," he said with a sweep of his arm.

"*Shukran*," I said. *Thank you.* I moved through the doorway, brochures clasped in my hand, and he closed the door behind me. Tense, not knowing what to expect from the man, I kept my eyes on

124

him while I took in my surroundings.

Without a word, he led the way down a hallway. I could hear a TV playing. A game show?

As we neared the entry, he spoke in Arabic. "We have company," he announced.

I looked in on ten Arab men lounging on chairs and sofas, seemingly enthralled by the TV. Their eyes turned to us, then settled on me. Some appeared puzzled, others grinned.

"This maiden has come to tell us about the Friday Mosque of Miami," the gatekeeper explained.

In response, I held my handful of brochures aloft.

One man turned the TV off, and silence settled on the room. Time for me to ad lib.

"I am a volunteer at the mosque, charged with spreading the word of our existence," I explained in Arabic. "Have any of you been to the mosque?"

I expected a universal shaking of their heads. One nodded yes. Fooled me.

Looking at him, I said, "I hope you found it satisfactory."

"Yes, yes. The imam led a fine service," he replied.

"Thank you for making my task easy," I said. "For those of you who have not been, I have a simple brochure that is filled with helpful information." I moved into the room and handed a brochure to each man, bypassing the man who'd said he'd been there. I started to turn away, but he spoke up.

"I'll take one, too, please."

"Certainly. I have more than enough for everyone," I said, and moved to give him one.

When I'd finished distributing the brochures, the room was silent save for the sound of papers being ruffled.

Mister Mosque-goer looked up and said, "Please excuse my bad manners. Come, sit with us," he invited, sweeping a hand at an empty chair. "My name is Ibraihim," he added, a mild smile playing on his mouth.

"I am Aiesha Ahmadi," I replied, bowing slightly as I spoke.

I padded across the floor and sat down, gathering my parahaan around me as I did so. That allowed me to reach into my pants pocket and fish out the bug without being obvious. Now I needed the opportunity to plant it.

Fumbling with the brochures, I let one drop to the floor. I leaned forward to retrieve it while my other hand stuck the mini mike on the underside of my padded chair. I sat straight again, pretending to be embarrassed at my clumsiness. Nobody showed the least interest. Good.

As I sat up, I started to tell the men more about the mosque.

The man who'd opened the door for me interrupted. "We are cautious men. Do you mind being searched?" His steely brown eyes bored into mine.

"It is a matter of modesty," I said, keeping my tone neutral. "I choose not to have men examine me."

"Sure. Sure. I will call Ibraihim's wife to perform the search."

He stood and hurried to a back room of the house, leaving the living room in total silence as the other nine men stared suspiciously at me.

At length he returned, a modestly dressed woman by his side.

She approached me, introduced herself as Fatimah, and told me how sorry she was that she must search me, then led me to the room she'd exited. She closed the door behind us.

I looked around the small bedroom that doubled as a sitting room, sparsely furnished with a double bed, two padded chairs and a table. A small lamp sat on the table. I spotted two bulky suitcases on the floor in the far corner. Fatimah and I were alone in the room.

"I must check you for a listening device, then verify your identification," she explained. It was clear she was embarrassed.

I nodded to her, then stripped off my hijab and parahaan. I stood before her wearing nothing but a bra.

"Please turn around," she instructed.

I turned slowly, showing her my sides and back, thankful we had decided not to have me wear a wire.

"Thank you. Please put your clothing back on. Again, I am so sorry for causing you embarrassment."

"Anything for Mohammed," I replied, thankful that her search hadn't included my pockets, where she would have discovered my folding knife. I pulled my parahaan over my head and wrapped my head in my hijab, pausing to make sure strands of hair hadn't snuck out.

"Here is my identification," I said, taking the cards from my purse and handing them to her.

She examined them carefully, one by one. Then she handed them back to me. "You have passed with flying colors," she announced, smiling warmly.

"Thank you," I replied, returning her smile.

She opened the door and led me to the main living room and the expectant men. "She is who she says she is, and she has no listening devices," she told the room.

All ten men visibly relaxed, smiled at one another.

I sat back in the chair I'd planted the bug under, breathing my own sigh of relief. I watched Fatimah return to her room, then spoke. "If any of you have any questions, I will do my best to answer them."

"Yes, tell me about the women's prayer room," asked the gatekeeper. I guessed he wanted to reassure himself that I knew the mosque, that I wasn't a spy, or worse.

"Certainly," I began. "Do you have a wife who might join us in the mosque?"

"Not me," he replied. "But there are those who do." Since I saw no other women, I assumed he meant Fatimah, Ibraihim's wife.

I described the women's prayer room in full detail, glad I'd thought to visit it. I described it right down to the design on the prayer carpet. When I finished, I could see that I had answered the gatekeeper correctly.

"Thank you for that," he said. "Tell us, what is your country of origin?"

"I am Afghani," I replied. "And what of all of you?"

"We are from many places," Ibraihim answered for everyone.

Another of the men found his voice. "Four of us are from Somalia," he informed me. "I am called Rahman Ali, and this is Jamaal Raage, and over there is Yusuf Warsam. There is Mohammed Ahmed," gesturing at each of his fellow Somalians as he identified them.

"It is a pleasure to make your acquaintances," I said, nodding to each in turn. "Are you all from the same town?"

The spokesman took his cue. "We are from Xuddur, which is in the Bakool region."

"Are you brothers? Connected by families?" I asked, making light conversation.

"Ah, a very good question. We are unaware of a family connection, but who knows? Fifty years ago, a hundred years ago, it is possible, because our last names are not the names of our fathers, and less than perfect records have been kept. We like to think of ourselves as brothers, and that is more likely than unlikely," he concluded, favoring me with a smile filled with stained teeth.

"You look like brothers and you act like brothers, so *inshallah*, you are," I said. *If God wills.*

All four men grinned, showing me their stained and broken teeth. We were getting along well, so I figured my next question would be easy for them.

"What brings you to America?" I asked.

A perceptible pause followed as the spokesman hesitated to answer, but he recovered quickly. "We have secured green cards and we are in search of work," he said, tossing in a wily smile for good measure.

"That is wonderful," I said, sitting slightly forward. "There is much work available here. No doubt you will have an easy time in finding employment."

"*Insha'Allah*," replied the spokesman, using my words.

I placed my hands together in front of my face and bowed towards him, offering a gesture of peace. I decided to change the subject. "Does anyone have any questions concerning the mosque or the services available?" I asked of all the men in the room.

Ibraihim reasserted himself. "The brochure you have given us is very thorough. I don't believe we have any questions. Do we?" he asked.

All heads shook negatively.

"If that is the case, I will leave you. With your permission, I will return in the morning to answer any questions that may form overnight." I glanced around for a sign.

"We will be happy to welcome you back in the morning, Aiesha Ahmadi," said Ibraihim. "Let me escort you to the door."

We walked together, he leading the way, me following subserviently behind.

At the door, I held out a few remaining brochures. I kept three for myself. "Please accept these for anyone else who may need one," I offered.

He took them from me, and opened the door.

I stepped out into the growing heat of Miami's mid-morning and the door closed tightly behind me. I drew in a deep breath and exhaled. All in all, I thought everything had gone well.

When Ibraihim told me that they would welcome me back in the morning, it suggested that the teams wouldn't be moving out until then. Or maybe he said so, and I'd find an empty building in the morning. No telling.

I strolled down the street toward the next house, then paused to glance back, assuring myself that I wasn't being followed. If any of them had suspicions about me, they'd likely try to follow me, see where I went from there. The street was empty.

Reassured I'd pulled it off, I continued to the corner and went to the building the FBI agents were using. Nick, standing sentinel, saw me, and opened the door.

I climbed the stairs to the room they watched from, and asked if they could pick up the transmission from the bug I'd planted.

"Yeah, it's coming through loud and clear. Can't understand them, though," said Will, the earphones on his head.

"Mind if I listen?" I asked.

He pulled the headset off. "Knock yourself out," he said, handing it to me.

They spoke in Arabic, no surprise. I listened intently, trying to discern a topic, a theme, a focus. At first it appeared to be general, some comments about me, one man saying I reminded him of a woman back home. Then he added that he hoped to meet her in Paradise. That got my attention. Paradise, and what waited there was a common theme amongst terrorists willing to give their lives to promote the cause. Supposedly, 72 virgins will greet the martyr when he gets to Paradise. Now here's what I don't get. If a *jihadist* blows himself up for the cause, sending most of his body parts flying into the crowd, what shape will he be in to cozy up to one virgin, let alone 72? Maybe I'm missing something.

I continued to listen, hoping they'd discuss their plans, but the conversations stayed general, more of the same.

I glanced at Will, who'd been watching me the whole time. "You're recording all this, right?"

"Of course we are," he reassured me. That's when I noticed the recording device on the table.

"Can I listen to the early part while it's recording the new stuff?" I asked.

"The unit's got binary channels, so yeah, no problem," he explained.

I hadn't a clue what binary channels were, but I kept my ignorance to myself. "How do I listen to the earlier part?" I asked.

He pulled the headset jack from one port and plugged it into another, then flipped a switch. "You hear it?"

"Yes, thanks," I replied.

I listened to my conversation with the men, then me leaving, then the conversation that followed immediately after.

One man said, "She seems nice."

Then a second one said they should ask me about Afghanistan, make sure I turned out to be who I said I was.

A third said that made sense, suggested someone contact the mosque and verify that I volunteered there. Uh oh.

I pulled off the headset and took out my phone. When I got Yukon, I told him what my bug had revealed, could he have someone at the mosque vouch for me if a call came in? He told me he'd take care of it.

Relieved, I sat down and got comfortable.

I listened to the occasional mindless chatter, the TV playing in the background, and then to long blocks of silence as boredom settled over the terrorists, and over me. Minutes passed. Hours passed.

I remembered the last time Paul and I had shared meaningful moments together. He'd completed his Special Forces training and was awaiting orders to ship out. There wasn't any question about where he was going. Everyone in his team knew they were deploying to Afghanistan. Their training told them that. Running up and down mountains, practicing insertions from helos, everything they did pointed to Afghanistan as their destination. The only missing piece was the date and location of their departure.

Since the route to Afghanistan nearly always included a stop at an airfield in Germany, their departure would be from the east coast, so he couldn't stray far from Eglin, his assigned base. We arranged to meet in our old South Carolina digs, which brought our families together as well. He got to kill two birds with one stone, so to speak. He could spend time with his parents and younger brother at the same time I was sharing time with my parents and brother.

Our families may have felt cheated by the amount of time Paul and I were together, but they never complained to either of us. They had long ago accepted our relationship, and took our time together in stride.

The knowledge that Paul would soon leave for duty in a war zone and all the dangers and uncertainties waiting there for him brought us together. Each moment spent became intensified by the realization that he could leave and never return. I cherished every touch, every kiss, making love as if it were the last time. Paul's body had been honed to a magical combination of muscle and movement, and when we came together we were left breathless, shaken to our cores by the intensity we shared.

When his orders came through, we accepted our looming separation, and whispered promises of love and steadfastness to one another. Both of us recognized that the elephant in the room was the possibility that this might be our last time together, but we pushed it away to avoid the pain it brought with it. I missed him dearly.

My musings got interrupted by an agent announcing the arrival of a visitor to the terrorists' safe house. I stood and crept to the window, peered down at Lieutenant Lopez waiting for the door to open.

Interesting.

The door opened, he went in, and the door closed.

I strained to hear what he said, made difficult, no impossible, because he didn't go down the hall to the room where I'd hid the bug. The man he talked to spoke in a low voice, like he didn't want to be overheard, and Lopez followed suit.

He didn't stay five minutes.

The door opened, he ducked out and moved quickly to his cruiser.

When he'd gone, I asked Will if he could turn up the volume.

"Nope. Maybe the lab can, but I don't have that capability."

I thanked him, went back to listening, thinking Lopez's visit might provoke conversation.

It didn't. Nobody said a word about his showing up. Strange.

My phone told me it was almost noon. The third and final rendezvous was less than forty hours away. Time ticked away like a snail out for a morning stroll. Out the window, I saw a black sedan drive by the doorway, then pull to the curb and stop. When the brakes went on, I noticed the left tail light was out. Coincidence? Maybe.

I watched as two men climbed out and made their way to the doorway, their eyes everywhere but on the door as they approached. Then I spotted coincidence number two. The lead man wore ugly neon green and gold sneakers. No longer a coincidence. Stun Gun Man, no question about it. The door opened and they went inside.

"Can you read the plate on the sedan?" I asked Agent Will.

His fingers danced on a key pad. "Already did. I'm getting it run."

"Let me know what you find." I turned my attention to the headset, heard vague mumbling that seemed to be getting louder. Maybe this time the visitors would go to the living area and not hang back and talk in the hallway. I crossed my fingers and listened intently.

Two voices came through. One had to be Ibraihim. I guessed the other was Stun Gun Man. His silent partner continued to play his part. They spoke in hushed tones. I could decipher one word in three. I heard *vans*, then *vests*, then *four to*, then *ready*, then *allahu akbar*, followed by another *allahu akbar*. The last two phrases, 'God is great,' loud and clear, obviously spoken with force.

Immediately after, the door opened and Stun Gun Man and his silent partner stepped out, walked back to their car, their heads on swivels, and drove off. I took a deep breath, reassuring myself that I was safe. Once again, I shook off the memory of the assault.

"You okay?" Will had seen my expression change.

"Yeah, fine." I told Will and Nick what I'd heard. We puzzled over the words together. Vans seemed clear. The terrorists would be leaving in vans. Vests could mean explosive vests.

We got hung up on *four to*. Four to what? Four to a van? That made sense if you counted two terrorists, a handler and a driver in each van. Four people in four vans totaled sixteen in all. Four of them were drivers, so twelve would come from the building. In the past, terrorists had either acted alone or had a single handler. This time a handler would go along to make sure the nuclear devices got detonated properly. All possible.

Time to call Yukon.

After I told him the cryptic clipped words I'd heard, he admitted he had nothing further to add. He asked Nick to bring in the recording so it could be examined in the audio lab.

Will put in a new cd to continue recording anything new spoken, and Nick left to take the first cd to the experts at headquarters.

I returned to my listening and watching post, glad I'd eaten a good breakfast. No telling how long it'd be until my next meal.

My eyes stayed glued to the door across the street, but my mind strayed elsewhere. I found myself wondering where Paul was, what he might be doing. I'd run into him once in Afghanistan. I had been returning from a mission, he embarking on one. He'd spotted me on the tarmac, shouted my name, and rushed to meet me.

I saw the old spark there, a hint that he still cared. A jumble of words spilled out of both of us, intermingling, making no sense, really, though raw emotion filled the space between us like a tsunami, sending shock waves into both of us.

We never had the luxury of kissing. His commander yelled at him to get his ass on the helo, and he turned and ran to join his team at the waiting helicopter. An agonizingly brief encounter, but I clung to the memory.

After that brief meeting, my team got transferred to Jalalabad while Paul and his team stayed in Kabul. Worlds apart, as it turned out.

My mind wandered back to our high school days together, to the school-organized contest that was meant to determine who was the best in hand-to-hand combat. Paul was a junior, eleven months older than me. I was a sophomore. I knew who he was, and I guessed he knew who I was, but we'd never officially met, never dated. Both of us had benefited from our father's instructions, since they were both in Special Forces.

Somehow, I came out the winner in the school contest, besting Paul with a sudden move that caught him off-balance. I remember his smile and his little bow, acknowledging my victory.

Afterwards, we'd met and practiced our skills on each other on a regular basis, each of us getting better and better as we learned the strengths and weaknesses of each other's bodies. I was attracted to him right away, but Paul maintained a certain distance from me. Since he knew my father, it took time for him to make a move. When our inevitable union took place, it began a new relationship, a totally different form of give and take, and one we both shared fully.

Paul graduated and went off to college, leaving me alone in my senior year, our days together reduced to visits home on school breaks. Then I graduated and moved on to college, and Paul joined the army.

Suddenly we were worlds apart.

When Paul joined the US Army to become a Green Beret, I began wondering if he had always let me win our sparring contests, right from our first fight in the school contest. I'll never know for sure. Unless Paul admits to it. But would I believe him?

My attention got drawn back to the doorway below me. A black sedan with a pizza store emblem attached to the roof pulled up and stopped. The driver climbed out with several pizza boxes in hand, and strode up to the doorway. He rang the doorbell and waited. The door opened, and he stepped in without hesitation.

All sorts of bells were going off in my head. One, that wasn't a typical pizza delivery car. Two, the driver hadn't had on a shirt or cap identifying his pizza brand. And three, he'd walked in like he owned the place. I listened intently for a conversation through the headset, hoping for some clarification.

At first, the voices were faint. I guessed Pizza Man was carrying the pizzas through to the living area.

I heard a general surge of voices as the men spotted the pizza boxes and rushed forward. Then they died down while they worked their way through the food.

Pizza Man spoke in a confident tone, and Ibraihim responded in kind. Pizza Man said he'd arranged for four vans, two for each team. They would pull up to the building's doorway one-by-one to avoid attracting attention, and two men plus their handler would board each one. Each man would have a device. When loaded, they'd head off and the next van would pull up. The procedure would be repeated until everyone and each device had been loaded.

The vans would head out separately, two for Washington and two for New York. That way they would be much harder to detect, and if one van got stopped, the other would continue to the target and carry out the mission.

Ibraihim asked how they should carry the devices, since at present they were in two huge suitcases.

Pizza Man told him he'd bring him four plain boxes, big enough that two devices could be transferred into each. He said he'd go over the targets with the handlers when he came back.

Their voices began to fade as I visualized them walking to the front door.

The door opened, and Pizza Man returned to his car without so much as a sidelong glance. I guessed he felt confident in his disguise. He should have known better.

Will kept busy shooting pictures of him, coming and going. I knew he'd transmit them to FBI headquarters where they'd be run through the extensive database. If Pizza Man had a past, they'd ID him.

After I watched the man drive off, I picked up my phone and called Yukon to fill him in. He listened to my review without interruption.

"Looks like we were right. Two teams are heading out before the final team gets here. The question is, when? Today or tomorrow? Any thoughts?"

"Well, sir, it's a thousand miles to DC, and if they average 60 miles an hour, it'll take them around eighteen hours to get there. New York's about 1300 miles, and at 60 it'll take them 21 or 22 hours. If they leave today, they'll get to DC tomorrow, and to New York later, but sometime tomorrow. If I had to guess, I'd say they'll leave tomorrow, and arrive Saturday. Saturday's a good day to set off their devices, make their statement. That way the team coming in tonight can get out there Saturday and do their Miami thing, coordinated with the other two. It also takes away the waiting time, when an observant person could become suspicious of a couple vans parked together, engines idling."

"I agree. Leaving tomorrow makes more sense than leaving today, but we should be prepared to intercept them today if they head out sooner. The thing is, we need to come up with a plan to intercept them that can go down fast so they don't have time to detonate their devices. I'll work on it from here with my team. You let me know if you have any ideas. We'll talk soon."

He'd left me with a huge question. How do you take down eight terrorists in four different vehicles with eight separate devices, likely nuclear? One thing for sure: speed would be the key to success. Speed and surprise. We had to prevent them from detonating their weapons before we had them neutralized.

Hitting them while they were still in one place was logical. Trying to track down and overpower four vans in four different locations as they headed for their target cities made the least sense. So how do we go about taking down a house full of terrorists and their nasty weapons? I remembered my promise to return tomorrow to answer

134

any additional questions about the mosque. With me on the inside, perhaps a takedown at that time would be doable.

I called Yukon to get his opinion. He listened as I explained my thinking. When I'd finished, he asked, "So you're expected back tomorrow morning sometime?"

"Yes, that's correct," I said.

"My concern is that they'll leave before then, or after. You've got a narrow window that might work, but most likely won't. If they're planning their departure when you show up, they're likely to tell you to come back in a little while, to get you clear while they take off," Yukon reasoned.

"I see your point, sir," I conceded. "Let me think on it some more."

"Do that, EZ."

I heard his phone click off before I could respond, though what I could've said escaped me. He was right. They wouldn't want some female mosque-promoter hanging around while they divvied up the explosive devices and split their numbers amongst four vans. I knew one thing, for sure. If a van pulled up, we needed to be ready to move, and fast. Thinking, I went to the bathroom and changed out of my Aisha duds. Emerging, I had an idea.

"What do you want on your pizza?" I asked Will and Nick.

They looked at each other, then back to me, smiling, understanding where I was going with it. They told me their favorite ingredients.

"One family-size pizza, coming up!" I said, already on my way to the door.

I wanted to check out the pizza shop Mister Pizza Man had come from, remembering the address on the sign mounted to his car's roof. Its location took me north towards Miramar, maybe two miles south of FBI headquarters. I wondered if Yukon or any of his agents got their pizza there.

When I got to the address, I guessed they didn't.

Surprise. No pizza shop, unless the second-hand store at that address sold pizza. I searched the area for the black sedan with the pizza sign on top, but it was nowhere to be found.

I turned around and headed to the stakeout, detouring slightly to stop at a pizza parlor I knew from previous visits. I waited while they baked my order, then returned to the stakeout building, the aroma teasing me all the way back.

After parking on a side street, I had a good look around to make sure nobody found my arrival interesting. Reassured that I had the street to myself, I grabbed the pizza box and the family-size bottle of cola, and made my way back.

Will and Nick greeted my arrival with obvious enthusiasm, their eyes locked onto the pizza box.

Nick asked, "What took you so long?"

I waited for him to add, "We were worried about you," but the follow-up never came. The pizza had captured their undivided attention.

I held my hand on the top of the box while I told them what I'd found at the so-called pizza shop address, then asked if they'd gotten any information on the pizza car's registration number. They had.

"Let me guess," I said. "It's registered to Gofish Corporation?"

"How'd you know?" Will asked, surprised.

"It's come up before. Dummy corporation. These guys are organized," I added grimly. "Let's eat."

I held the cardboard cover up while Will and Nick swooped in. I'd made two loyal friends. Until the next meal, anyway.

I sat back and considered my next move. We were at a disadvantage, not knowing when the vans would start pulling up and loading, and once they started, they could be on their way fast. Five minutes per van max, they could be northbound in twenty minutes. Once on the road, they'd be much harder to find and stop. Four targets, scattered across the interstate system.

Hitting them here and now, while they were still in the building, had its drawbacks, too. The third team could be alerted and diverted, and could come ashore sometime later to carry out their attack.

With these thoughts rattling around in my head, the door opened and Agent Rick Brophy hobbled in, supported by a hospital-issue cane. His appearance caught me off guard.

"Hey, Rick, you're looking good."

"Hey yourself, EZ. Special Agent Yukon tells me you've been busy."

"We all have," I said, a sweep of my arm including the other two agents as a way of drawing us together.

"Do these guys know how good you are with your hands?" he asked, glancing from me to Will to Nick.

"What do you mean, sir?" asked Nick.

"This young lady could put either one of you, or both of you for that matter, on your asses before you could even think about it," Brophy said. "She's good."

"That so?" Nick replied, eyeing me.

"Yes. That's so," confirmed Brophy, his big grin spreading across his face.

Nick moved fast, I'll give him that, but he started off-balance in his attack. Not a good way to begin. He lunged at me, so I let his momentum carry past me, then swept his feet, dropping him unceremoniously on his butt at my feet.

Will moved on me when Nick went down, trying to catch me off balance, unprepared. He didn't fool me. When he cocked his right arm to roundhouse me, I stepped into him, clamped onto his arm.

He straightened the arm to deliver his blow, but I used his momentum to roll his body off my hip and onto the floor, doing my best to ease his impact.

"See what I mean?" asked Brophy, grinning widely at the results his taunting had brought on.

I pulled Will up to his feet, alert for a counterattack. It never came.

I reached down to give Nick a boost back up. He stared at me a moment, then accepted my hand. Once upright, he looked me in the eye and said, "Nice move." No malice, no hard feelings. The way it should be.

"Thanks," I replied, holding his eyes with mine, ready in case he had more for me. He didn't.

Nick and Will returned to their observations at the window as if nothing had happened. Pros.

Brophy pulled out a chair at the table and got himself seated. "Come. Sit," he said, gesturing to me to sit across from him. "Give me a sit-rep."

I reviewed what had happened so far and the thoughts I'd had about how to handle the situation. When I'd finished, he said, "Yeah, we're damned if we take them out here, and double-damned if we let them get on the highway."

"What's your best guess as to the type of devices they'll try to use?" I asked.

"Probably dirty bombs, not actual nuclear bombs," he replied levelly.

"So, less destruction, but loads of psychological impact."

"Exactly. Nuclear bombs are heavy and require detonation devices like krytrons, damned hard to get. Dirty bombs can be put together with U-235 or U-232, any kind of refined uranium or plutonium, wrapped around symtex or a similar explosive. When the explosive goes off, the U-232 or U-235 gets blasted into the surrounding air and contaminates everything it lands on for a long time."

"I can picture the effect it'd have on Wall Street, or on the Capitol in Washington. The world's biggest financial market would cease to exist, and at the same time, the American government would come to a standstill."

"You got it, EZ. We've got to stop these bastards, one way or another."

"Question is, how?" I asked.

"Agent Yukon has a plan together to put locator devices on the vans, then we'll pick them off one by one on their drive north. Find spots when they're isolated, hit them fast."

"Surprise works. How's he getting the locator devices on the vans?" I asked Brophy, my brows furrowed, puzzled.

Brophy stared back at me in silence, his face serious.

"Why are you looking at me like that?" I asked, then realization struck home. "That's my job, right? Guess I should be asking how?"

"That's the longest I've ever heard you speak, EZ," Brophy said, his stare replaced by a grin.

I ignored his remark, already working on a plan. "What if I'm there when they head out, a farewell party of one, so to speak? I could plant a locator on each van as it's loading. I told them I'd stop by to see if any of them had questions about the mosque anyway."

"How could you plant the devices without arousing suspicion?"

"Well, if they head out before my visit tomorrow morning, I'll walk over there with four magnetic locators in my pants pocket and act like I'm surprised they're leaving, can I say goodbye. As each van pulls up, I'll stick a locator on it, then wave good-bye and wish them well."

I shifted in the chair, another idea coming to me. "If they haven't left before I visit in the morning, I hope to get some of them to go to the mosque with me. It's Friday, their holy day, so I'm guessing some of them will want to have one last mosque visit. That'd give us a common ground, I'd be more trusted by them. Afterwards, I'll do my best to get one of them to tell me when they're leaving, and I'll show up to say good-bye with the locators in my pocket."

"It's a viable plan. Dangerous for you, but possible. I'm impressed," Brophy said. "If there's problems with it, we'll move to Plan B. One of the agents will go up to the building's roof and fire a paintball at each of the van's roofs. The paintballs they use are full of a bright paint that contains florescent dye, so it'll be visible from above, night or day. Only problem is the sound it'll make, hitting the van roof. If someone alerts to the sound and looks at the van's roof, it's over."

"Let's bet on Plan A, Rick," I said, sounding more confident than I was. So many things could go wrong.

"By the way, I brought the locators and the paintball gear. They're out in my car."

Taking his cue to leave, Will followed Brophy down to his car to retrieve the gear. I looked down at the safe house and hoped I had the luxury of time to carry out my plan. I preferred 'hurry up and wait' to 'rush to get it done.' Haste could be full of consequences. Deadly ones.

Nick stayed behind. He was the one who'd ended up sitting down hard, and he asked me where I'd learned my combat skills.

I told him.

"I don't feel so bad now. I got taken down by a pro!"

I laughed. "Thanks. Don't forget, Rick tricked you into trying something on me. It could happen to anyone."

"No hard feelings," he said, extending his hand.

I took it warily, prepared for a trick move, but he offered none. Sensing his sincerity, I returned his strong shake.

We heard the returning agent at the door, and turned to face it. Will came in with two boxes in his arms. He set them on the table, then handed the smaller one to me.

I opened it and found six magnetic GPS locators, each about the size of a nickel. Miniaturization. It keeps getting better all the time. They were painted flat white, the expected color of the vans. They'd send out a steady signal strong enough to be picked up by a drone, by a low-flying aircraft or by a trailing vehicle, a signal unique to them and them alone. Once detected, a trailing vehicle could close in on them.

I set the box on the table with the other one, not wanting to pocket them until game time. Now it truly was 'hurry up and wait' time.

A surprise visitor stopped out front less than a half hour later. Lopez stepped from his black sedan and moved quickly to the suspects' doorway. I still didn't understand why he was working with the terrorists.

Didn't matter. If he was part of it, he had to be taken down, too. I had an idea. Brophy'd given me six locators, so I had two extras.

I grabbed one from the box and dashed out the door and down the stairs, leaving Will and Nick to wonder what I was up to.

I turned the corner and crossed the street to Lopez's cruiser. With a stumble and a clumsy recovery, I put the locator on the underside of his rear bumper, then continued past the building, circling the block and ending at our stakeout.

When I was safely back inside, I glanced out the window to see Lopez's cruiser gone. Another quick visit. I hit 9-1-1, got Yukon, and told him what I'd done.

"Nice work," he said. "I'll get a detail to track him, find out what he's up to."

Exactly what are you up to, Lieutenant Lopez?

Sitting there in my comfortable western clothes, I asked myself how Muslim women tolerated the constriction a hijab placed on their heads and necks. And for the umpteenth time, I concluded that anything could become tolerable over time.

A car stopped outside the terrorists' doorway, bringing me away from my musings. I watched as Stun gun Man and his partner hurried to the door.

I ran for the door, another locator clutched in my hand.

I pulled my stumble and clumsy recovery act again, and slapped the magnetic locator on the underside of Stun Gun Man's sedan.

Someone stepped into my path.

A woman. I recognized her as the woman from the first house I'd knocked on, the one who had slammed the door in my face. I prayed she didn't recognize me without my Arab clothing. She didn't give me a second glance.

Relieved, I casually strolled past her without making eye contact and back to the stakeout in time to see the two men leave the building, crane their necks all round, and get back in their sedan. Once they were out of sight, I called Yukon to give him the news.

"Way to go, EZ. I'll get another team together to track them. You need more locators?"

"I've got four left. Unless there's another vehicle we need to track, I'm good, sir."

"Let me know."

He'd hung up before I could respond. Man didn't mince words. Checked the clock. Four-fifteen. Tick-tock. Hurry up and wait.

***

My phone rang. Yukon. Asked me if I wanted to take a drive.

"Both Lieutenant Lopez and Stun Gun Man drove to the dock where the suspects' boat is kept. Go there in your casuals and see what you can find out."

I told Will and Nick what I was doing and that I'd return soon. They acknowledged with waves and I beat it out to my car.

As I turned into the parking area at the head of the dock, I passed a black SUV parked beside the access turn, two men sitting inside. I guessed they were monitoring the locators. I passed them, then parked next to Lopez's cruiser. He wouldn't recognize my Fiat since I drove my VW when working at the Adriatic. I hoped my auburn hair would be enough to keep him from recognizing me.

I headed down the dock, keeping the one across from me in my periphery. When I reached the boat, I stepped aboard, my eyes busy sweeping for any changes since I'd left. Signs of an intruder.

A blind man couldn't have missed the mess.

The cabin had been tossed. Lures and fishing gear were strewn across the floor. My neat little boxes had been ripped apart, the lures and foam scattered across the cabin floor. I didn't think anything was missing, but everything had been checked. If it had been mine, I'd have been furious. In any case, relief trumped anger. I still needed to play the part, though.

I turned to the cockpit, swearing loudly for all to hear. I looked across to the suspect's boat and saw Lopez, Stun Gun Man, and his bodyguard standing alongside it.

"Hey, you guys!" I shouted at them. "Did you see anyone messing around my boat?" I pitched my voice differently to keep them from recognizing me, and tilted my head down to obscure their view of my face. None of them had seen my auburn hair. If I'd been closer, I swear I could've seen smiles on their faces.

"No!" shouted Stun Gun Man. "Why?"

"Someone's thrown all my fishing gear around, made a hell of a mess!" I yelled back.

"Anything missing?" he asked. Interesting question, since I guessed he already knew the answer.

"I don't know yet. Haven't taken inventory!"

"Probably a friend pulling a prank on you," he suggested.

I swear I could see a grin on his ugly face.

"Yeah, right! Some friend!" I shot back.

They went back to whatever I'd interrupted, showing no signs of recognizing me, and I spent ten minutes looking to see if anything was missing. One thing I knew. If they'd found anything incriminating, they'd have come for me. Their lack of interest told me they hadn't.

I carried a tackle box and a handful of gear to the cockpit, sat down on the engine cover, and busied myself with sorting and organizing the mess. With my baseball cap pulled low, I had a clear view of the suspect boat and its three visitors.

They stood in a circle, talking in low tones, all very innocent looking to the casual eye. I knew better.

I picked up my phone, called Yukon. Told him quietly about the search of my boat and the three men standing by the suspects' boat. Asked him to send police to check out the vandalism on my boat, and could he get them to bring me a receiver/recorder so I could hear what they were saying through the bugs I'd planted earlier.

"Where's the tablet?" he asked.

"At the apartment. Never thought of it when I left."

"Yeah, why would you? I'll get a recorder to you," said Yukon, then disconnected.

Less than ten minutes later a police cruiser pulled into the lot and two uniforms made their way down the dock to me, their eyes searching.

I watched the three men for reaction, saw Lopez turn his back in my direction. Seems he didn't want to be recognized. Otherwise, the circle remained unbroken.

The officer in front reached my boat, and asked, "Aiesha Ahmadi?"

"That's me. Thanks for coming. Someone went through all my stuff. Made a huge mess," I explained.

"Anything taken?" he inquired.

"Not sure."

"We'll have a look around, file a report, make it official," he explained. "I was told to give this to you," he added, handing a mini-receiver/recorder to me.

"Thanks," I replied, taking it from him while checking to see if the three musketeers were watching us. They stood looking away at the sea, as before.

The two officers stepped aboard my boat, then ducked into the cabin to examine the mess. Their response was a slight shaking of their heads.

After a moment, they came out. The officer in charge made eye contact, and said, "Probably kids. School vacation this week, they're bored, nothing to do. See this kind of stuff all the time. Let us know if you find anything missing." He handed me his card and they left. No sense wasting any more time over something as trivial as this.

If they only knew.

I sat down on the engine cover, my hands full, and made myself look busy sorting lures while I turned on the radio receiver/recorder. It had a voice-activated recorder so it'd only run when voices came through. A low mumbling of voices came from it. The trio were standing too far away from the bugs for proper transmission. They'd have to climb on board for me to pick up a decent signal, and I doubted that was going to happen.

One of the trio turned and strode up the dock, headed to shore. I recognized Lieutenant Lopez. Stun Gun Man and his bodyguard watched him go, then climbed aboard the boat. I turned to the receiver, listening.

"I don't trust that cop," said Stun Gun Man. I knew that voice only too well. Imprinted permanently into my memory banks.

"What're you thinkin', boss?"

"Thinkin' a cop'd be crazy to want his town blown up," Stun Gun replied.

"Yeah, that's funny. Funny strange, not funny ha ha," corrected his bodyguard.

"Yeah, I got it," he said, sarcasm dripping from his voice.

"So whatcha wanta do, boss?"

"For now we watch, see if he gives himself away. Let's go."

That ended the conversation as they climbed off the boat and headed along the dock for shore.

I didn't think, after the thorough search they'd given my boat, they'd come back for another search, so I felt comfortable leaving the recorder on board. It fit nicely in one of the rod holders on the cabin roof. Long as it didn't rain, it'd be fine. The weather forecast for the next couple days called for sunshine, so I wasn't worried. In forty-eight hours, this'd all be over. One way or another.

I made my way up the dock and to my parked car. The SUV was gone, likely tailing either Lopez, or Stun Gun Man and his bodyguard.

I took the precaution of walking around the car, looking for anything that didn't belong on or under it. A bomb would be a bad sign. A locator wouldn't be good, either. I found nothing. Relieved, I got in and headed to the stakeout.

I sensed strain, anxiety between the two agents as I opened the door and stepped inside. Something had happened.

"What?" I asked them, my eyes searching their faces for a clue.

"The agents who followed those two guys from the dock were ambushed. The driver's dead, his partner's wounded," Will explained.

"Shit! Was there a second vehicle?"

"Not sure. They won't be able to question the wounded agent until he's out of surgery."

That made two strikes on Stun Gun Man and his genius bodyguard. I hoped I'd be around when they got taken down.

I changed the painful subject. "Nothing new across the way?"

"Nope. No visitors since you left, and nobody's come out," Nick said.

"That's good," I said.

Silence settled over us. I took the opportunity to change into my Arab clothes. I wanted to be ready if a van showed up.

Will's phone trilled, breaking the silence.

He answered, listened, then said, "Good, sir. I'll pass the word," and ended the call.

"The agent's out of surgery. He'll make a full recovery. He told Agent Yukon the car they were following somehow got behind them, then pulled up alongside and opened fire."

I shook my head. One man dead, but thankfully, the other would live to see another day. I shared what Stun Gun Man and his friend had done to me, leaving out the details. "I hope to be there when he goes down."

"I hear you," Will and Nick responded as one.

***

The light started to fade as the February sun settled in the west. The clock said it was nearly six. The door opened and two fresh agents stepped inside. One held a paper bag. They introduced themselves to me. A young Hispanic named Alberto and a thirtyish, balding man named Jack.

Will and Nick summarized what had happened over the past twelve hours. Shift change. Nobody taking my place. I wondered idly when overtime began for me.

After the door closed on Will and Nick, Alberto raised the paper bag. "Dinner. Hope you like tuna."

"Sounds good," I replied, thinking this would be my second seafood dinner in a row.

Alberto upended the bag, and three submarine sandwiches slid out onto the table, together with three bags of chips. "Dig in," he said, pushing one in my direction.

I looked up at him. "What're you guys going to eat?"

For a second he stared down at me, then at the sandwiches, his mouth dropping. Gradually, a smile spread across his face. "Ah, you got me!"

"Yeah, I did," I replied.

We each grabbed a sandwich and bag of chips, silence settling over our feast.

"Nice," I mumbled after I swallowed a bite.

"It's on Agent Yukon's tab," Alberto told me, wiping mayo off his lip.

Jack stood sentinel at the window, looking down on the suspects' doorway as he munched.

I finished, balled up my wrapper and chip bag into one and shot it at the waste basket in the corner. Swish! Two points!

Alberto, watched, did the same, with the same result. Tie game.

Jack joined in, dropped his in, too. We had us a contest. One problem: we were out of game balls. To be continued…

We took turns watching, a half hour on, an hour off. The safe house stayed quiet. No visitors, no departures. At ten, I was ready to examine the inside of my eyelids, told Alberto and Jack I needed some shut eye. I made sure to ask that they wake me up if anything happened, then got horizontal on the couch.

It'd been a long day, but I couldn't get my brain to turn off. I kept thinking of different situations, of all the things that could go wrong. How would I improvise? Three cities depended upon me and my actions against the terrorists.

Chapter Eleven

Day Eleven—Friday

A knock at the door startled me. Instantly awake, I lurched upright on the couch, struggling to recall where I was and how I got there. I got my bearings in time to see Will and Nick arriving for their twelve-hour shifts. Nick carried a paper bag. Breakfast had arrived. Wish I could be somewhere to make my own, but that wasn't happening now.

Alberto and Jack debriefed Will and Nick on the nothing night we'd had, and I fist-bumped Alberto and Jack out the door.

Nick opened the paper bag, and took out three large coffees from a cardboard tray, plus three breakfast sandwiches from the bag, arranging everything in three separate spaces. "Agent Yukon said enjoy your breakfast," Nick said. "Anything can happen today."

After a restless night, I was ready to refuel. I sat down at the table, a coffee and sandwich in front of me. The coffee was black, the way I liked it. The sandwich was nasty—with egg, cheese, and sausage crammed inside a big, flaky biscuit. Also the way I liked it.

Enough coffee remained for me to sip. I balled up my wrapper and made another 2-point shot. Will took the challenge and sunk his, and Nick, on window duty, did the same. We awarded him three points for his longer shot. Window duty had its bennies.

The waiting game continued.

I broke it up with bathroom time that included washing my face and hands, and brushing my teeth with a finger. Better than nothing. I combed through my hair with a small comb from my purse, and applied lip gloss. I wished I'd had the foresight to pack deodorant or perfume, too.

The clock hands crept inexorably around to eight-thirty, the time when I figured the terrorists would be up and ready for my promised visit. I told Will and Nick what my plans were, grabbed a handful of mosque brochures from the table for effect, left the locators behind in case I got searched again, and headed down the stairs wrapped in my hijab.

At the street door, I opened it quietly and peered out, checking in both directions. The coast was clear. I stepped out and strolled to the corner that took me to the suspects' doorway. Nobody stood outside. Good.

I reached the door and pushed the doorbell, then knocked for good measure.

Fifteen, thirty seconds passed.

I raised my hand to knock again but stopped, hearing footsteps approaching the door from the inside. I sensed an eye looking at me through the peephole. The locks turned and the door swung open.

Ibraihim looked down on me, smiling in recognition. "*Salaam alaikum*, young lady. I see you remembered to come back."

That seemed a strange thing to say. "*Walaikum salaam.* Indeed I did," I said. "Have you added any more to your numbers?"

"No, we remain the same."

"Since today is Holy Friday, perhaps some among you would like to attend the noon service, *Jumu'ah*. I would consider it an honor to lead the way," I said.

"Oh, please excuse my lapse in hospitality. I have much on my mind. Come, we will ask if anyone wants to go to the service." He gestured me down the hall to the living room.

Halfway there, he turned to me and said, "You were given a glowing report when I called the mosque to inquire after you."

"That is always good to hear," I replied. Inwardly, I expelled a sigh of relief. Agent Yukon had worked his magic once again.

We reached the living area, and the same faces lifted to mine and smiled in recognition. Ibraihim told me to have a seat, he would get Fatimah to perform the usual search. "A formality," he said, spreading his hands by way of apology.

I waited in silence, knowing that speaking before the search was conducted would be offensive.

He returned with Fatimah at his side. She smiled at me and beckoned for me to follow her. She led me to the same room, the room that also contained the two bulky suitcases. She closed the door behind me and asked me to remove my upper clothing, as before.

I did so, standing there half naked, except for my bra.

As she examined me for a wire, I noticed her hands trembling. She looked pale.

"Are you feeling well, Fatimah?" I asked.

"It is nothing," she replied. "A touch of the flu, perhaps."

A touch of radiation poisoning, perhaps. My eyes fell on the two bulky suitcases in the corner.

"Thank you for tolerating my search once again. It is Aiesha, is it not?"

"It is indeed," I replied, smiling. "Thank you, Fatimah, for remembering my name. That means much to me."

"You do me the same honor by remembering *my* name." She beamed at me.

I replaced my *parahaan* and rearranged my *hijab*.

"You look fine," she told me. "Come. I will escort you back to the gathering."

"Perhaps you would honor me by joining me at the mosque service, Fatimah."

"Why thank you, Aiesha. That is so thoughtful of you." She reached out and grasped my hands, blushing with pleasure.

She led the way to the living area, and I sat once more in the assigned chair. I saw her exchange a nod and glance with Ibraihim.

He sat down and addressed the group. "As you can see, Aiesha has returned to us as she promised. If anyone has a question about the mosque, now is the time to ask."

A hand reached up.

"Yes?" I responded.

"Today is Holy Friday," began a swarthy-looking Arab man. "Is there a service we might attend?"

"Indeed there is," I replied. "There is the main service, *Jumu'ah*, that takes place at the noon hour. I have agreed to lead as many of you who wish to attend through the streets to the mosque. The journey will take us no more than ten minutes."

The man turned to Ibraihim. "Will we have the time to make such a trip?"

Ibraihim looked at me. "What time do you expect to return here?"

"The service takes about an hour, and there is a lunch of good Arab food after, for those who wish to partake. I would say that we will easily return here by two-thirty, perhaps sooner," I said.

"Then you have my permission to make the trip," Ibraihim told the swarthy Arab. "Keep track of time, make sure you return by three o'clock at the latest."

"I will make certain that your wishes are fulfilled," I told Ibraihim, bowing my head in his direction.

"We thank you, Aiesha," Ibraihim said.

"Let us plan to depart from here no later than eleven-thirty," I suggested. "Then we will have sufficient time to wash our feet, and everyone can have a look around the mosque before the start of the service. Are there others who will join us?" I asked the assembled group.

Every hand was raised.

"Oh, that is good! The *imam* will praise me for bringing you to his service," I exclaimed, clapping my hands together.

Ibraihim made eye contact with me. "Since we have the luxury of time, perhaps you can tell us how you made your way to the Great, er, United States."

Once again, I sensed that the Great Satan nearly raised his ugly head.

"I am happy to tell you," I began. "The United States is very generous towards the Afghanis whose family members are accidentally killed by their drones. Such is my situation. Both my father and brother were killed in such a strike. There were no Taliban or Al Qaeda present. It was a family gathering of the men, so my mother and I were safely away," I explained, looking down at the floor in front of me as I spoke in a low voice.

"That is a sad story, and even sadder because I have heard it repeated many times," said Ibraihim. "Tell me, Aiesha. Where was your home in Afghanistan?"

I was ready for that one. "I am from the Pech Valley, south of Nuristan. Curiously, there are people there who have blue eyes and blond hair. I received the blue eyes. My brother had blond hair," I said, arranging my clothing around me. "My people are Pashtun."

"How did you end up here in the United States?" prodded Ibraihim.

"Following the drone attack that killed my father and my brother, a representative of the US Government came to our village and apologized to us for their mistake. They offered to make all the arrangements necessary to bring my mother and me here. My mother chose to stay in the valley, the only home she has ever known. I chose to come here and start a new life," I said, glancing up at him. "There is not a day that goes by that I don't question my decision. The United States is a very foreign place to me, though the Arab community I have found here is very comforting, very supportive."

"They provided everything for you?" questioned Ibraihim.

"They did. They provided me with a green card, an identification card, a sum of money each month, and a ride on an air force transport plane to MacDill Air Force Base in Tampa. The base sent a refueling plane out to meet us over the Atlantic, and escorted us to the base. Once we landed, they quickly loaded me with six other Afghanis into a transport vehicle and brought us here to Miami. That was eight months ago," I explained to the attentive terrorists.

"The US Government's way of making themselves feel better about their deadly mistakes," commented Ibraihim.

"It is a strange land with much opportunity, but I am still a stranger here," I replied evenly.

"Have you ever felt like doing something to avenge the deaths of your father and brother?" he asked.

The room became silent, waiting for my response.

There it was: the big question I'd hoped for. I needed to answer carefully.

"I have, yes. There is much anger in my heart. But what can a young girl do? I feel weak in the face of the mighty United States," I said to the attentive listeners.

Smiles broke out across most of their faces.

"You are a kindred spirit, Aiesha," said Ibraihim. "We share your anger. Do not discount your weakness as a woman. There are many advantages to it. Most of those in authority ignore women as threats, which gives you the opportunity to get closer to a target than the average man," he explained.

He glanced at his watch. "But we will continue this discussion later. Now we must prepare our minds and bodies for the *masjid*, the mosque," he said, getting to his feet.

The eight terrorists stood as well, and set off to wash and prepare for the service, leaving me alone in the large empty living room with my thoughts.

It wasn't empty long. Fatimah emerged from her room and asked me if she could get me a cup of tea while I waited.

"That sounds lovely, Fatimah. Thank you," I said with enthusiasm.

"Follow me. The kitchen is through here."

She led the way to a tiny kitchen cluttered with the dirty dishes and doings of thoughtless men.

"Excuse the mess," she said, shaking her head at the clutter.

"I know it's not your mess," I said cheerfully.

"You are not only attractive, Aiesha. You are also observant," she replied, a sheen of sweat on her upraised face.

"I also see that you are not feeling well. I don't think it's the flu, Fatimah. I urge you to go to a doctor."

"Perhaps you are right. I will see what I can arrange."

She cleared a space on the counter, found two clean cups, and in no time, a kettle was singing on the stove. She used loose tea in a separate pot. After a brief wait to let it steep, she poured the tea into two cups. She led the way back to the living room, each of us with a cup in hand.

We sat and sipped our tea together. Fatimah recounted her life in Pakistan, and I told her of mine in Afghanistan, careful to mention the details I'd concocted for the men in case she'd been eavesdropping.

***

The men returned to the living area by 11:25, washed and neat in appearance, each wearing a *pakol*, a cap covering their heads. Seeing that everyone was present, I told them I was ready to make the journey.

Ibraihim led the way down the hallway and let us out into the Miami noonday sun. I assumed the lead, knowing Nick and Will watched from above.

The trip was a short one, three blocks one way and four blocks another. We arrived in front of the mosque with time to spare, though there were other worshippers lining up at the entrance to remove their shoes and wash their feet. I told them I would meet them after the service at the food line, and made my way to the women's entrance with Fatimah at my side.

My line was short. One woman ahead of me removed her shoes, put them in the locker, and sat to wash her feet. I followed behind, duplicating her actions. Done, I moved inside and took up a position on the large prayer rug, facing East and Mecca. Soft Arabic music played through the speakers scattered around the room. I felt like an interloper, out of place in this setting, though I'd learned the Muslim prayer sequences as part of my Arab instruction before beginning my tours in Afghanistan.

At just after noon, the music stopped and the *imam's* voice replaced it. We all stood to begin the service. He led us through the opening prayers, and then we sat while he gave his sermon.

I listened to see if he said anything that could be interpreted as anti-American, but heard nothing.

His sermon over, the service was concluded with more prayers and commitments to Allah and Islam. Afterwards, I joined ten other women as we moved through a connecting doorway to the men's prayer room, and through to the dining area. The men had filled their plates and found seats, so we were free to get in line and take what we wanted, bearing in mind that some of the men would want seconds.

With enough food on my plate to dull my appetite, I turned and walked to a long table where the terrorists had parked themselves. They glanced up from their plates to see me, recognized me with smiles, then returned to their meals.

Their last supper. Or so I hoped. I let them eat without interruption.

When I saw the last man finish, I reminded them that there was more food if anyone wanted it. Two men stood up to take me up on it.

At the same moment, the *imam* shuffled over to our table and addressed us in his booming voice. "I see many new faces among you, and wanted to welcome you to my *masjid*," he said, beaming at one and all.

All faces turned his way and returned his smile. Some murmured "Thank you, Imam."

He spotted me sitting next to Fatimah and approached. "Welcome, child," he said. "Do I know you?"

Uh oh.

I decided the best way out of this would be to go on the offensive. "Why yes, Imam. I am Aiesha Ahmadi. I volunteer to go out into the community and find Muslims newly arrived in our city, and bring them to the *masjid*," I explained, my eyes downward to show respect.

"By the looks of the faces at this table, you have done your work well," he replied. "Keep up your good work."

"Thank you, Imam."

He moved on, and I breathed a quiet sigh, relieved. Dodged a bullet.

When I saw that everyone had finished their meal, I suggested that we head back. It was nearly two, and I'd promised Ibraihim we'd return by two-thirty. Everyone stood, picked up their plates and glasses, and dropped them off at the kitchen pass-through. Then we returned to the prayer room and the men reclaimed their shoes, while Fatimah and I walked through to the women's prayer room to do the same. We met again outside.

"How good is your memory? Who would like to take the lead? Don't worry. If you make a wrong turn, I am here to steer you right," I said in a cheerful voice.

With that encouragement, many hands were raised.

"Let us go, then!" I told the group with a wave of my arm.

The leader set off in the right direction. Good sign, good start.

One of the men drifted back to walk by my side. Seeing him approach, Fatimah dropped back, allowing him to speak freely with me.

"Thank you, Aiesha, for showing your kindness to us. I can safely speak for everyone when I say that we appreciate all that you have done."

"Thank you for your kind words. What is your name?"

"It is Musa, but my name is of no consequence. Soon we will be martyring ourselves in a far-off place," he divulged to me.

"Are you prepared to make this sacrifice, Musa?"

"Yes, I am prepared. Like you, we have heard and seen much evil carried out by the Great Satan."

"Then I wish you well on your journey, Musa."

"Listening to you in our temporary home, I think that martyrdom may be in your future, Aiesha. Perhaps we will meet again in Paradise. I would consider it an honor to have you as one of my virgins."

I inwardly grimaced and kept my voice neutral. "One never knows about these things," I said. "When will you be leaving?"

"There are vans coming to pick us up today at four O'clock."

"That is soon," I said. "Perhaps I can be there to see your departure."

"If you could, I'm certain that all of us would be honored," Musa replied.

"As long as Ibraihim approves, I will be there."

The missing puzzle piece fell into place. When I heard "four to", listening to the tape, the rest of 'to-' had been lost. I realized he'd said 'Four to*morrow*.' It made perfect sense now.

Not surprisingly, the group led the way unerringly back to the safe house. I complimented them on a job well done and they filed inside. Ibraihim met me at the door, smiling as he checked his watch. "Thank you, Aiesha. You have done well."

"It was my pleasure," I said. "Besides, the *imam* was equally pleased to see all the visitors. With your permission, I shall return at four O'clock to bid everyone a successful journey."

His face darkened. "How have you learned that there will be a departure at four?" He stared at me, his eyes full of suspicion.

"The men were open with me, knowing how I feel about the United States. They told me they were leaving today at four O'clock on a journey. They told me nothing else," I said, keeping my voice matter-of-fact.

Ibraihim locked eyes with mine and stared, deep in thought.

Finally he shrugged his shoulders and said, "I can find no harm in that. Come back at four then, Aiesha."

"Thank you so much, Ibraihim. Please don't think unkindly towards the men. They were merely showing friendship towards me," I explained.

"What's done is done," he said, conceding. "Until four, then."

With that, he stalked into the living room, leaving me to find my own way out.

I stepped outside and closed the door behind me, then retraced my steps to the corner and to the doorway that led to the FBI stakeout after being certain I wasn't being watched or followed.

When I walked in, Will and Nick greeted me.

"You've had a busy time of it. What'd you learn?" asked Will.

"Departure time is at four," I said. "I'm guessing 'four to' was shortened from 'Four tomorrow' on the recording."

"Oh, yeah. I remember. Good work figuring that one," he said.

"So, here's the plan," I said, getting comfortable on the couch. "I'm going back over at three fifty-five. They know I'm coming to see them off. That'll give me the chance to stick a locator on each van as it rolls in, and cover my ass by pretending to be a send-off party. If I'm unable to get a locator on a van, I'll raise my right fist in the air. You'll be up on the roof with the paintball gun, and if you see my signal, hit the roof of the van with a paintball. Sound good?"

"Yeah, sounds like a good plan," Will replied, nodding his agreement.

"I'll call Agent Yukon, bring him up to date." I hit 9-1-1 on my keypad.

I got through right away, and explained the situation. Yukon listened without interruption.

"Nice going, EZ. I'll get four shadow vehicles ready to roll at four.

Each shadow vehicle will lock on to a van locator and follow that van, staying well back until they're clear of other traffic. When that happens, they'll close and fire on them, hopefully without causing any civilian casualties."

"Sounds good, sir. What about the bombs?"

"You said they're dividing them up, putting two in a box in each van, correct?"

"That's what I heard one of them say, yes sir."

"It's likely that they'll put the bomb box in the rear of the van, and the passengers will sit in front of it," Yukon reasoned.

"I agree. Sounds like the most logical scenario."

"So the shooters in the shadow vehicles will concentrate their fire in the forward part of the van for maximum effect. When the van comes to a stop, they'll run to it and secure the bombs, check for survivors. What do you think?"

"I think that's as good as we can get it, under the circumstances," I told him. "What about the third boatload coming in tonight?"

"Don't worry. I've got it covered," came his cryptic reply. He clicked off before I could ask him what he had planned.

***

At ten minutes til four, locators stowed in my pants pocket, I headed for the safe house. Will and Nick wished me luck. I started to tell them luck had nothing to do with it, that it had to do with how well you prepared yourself, how well you considered the possible scenarios, how alert you were to changes. Maybe luck worked for those who didn't consider those things, and it worked for those who bet on the flip of a coin. Problem is, with coin-flipping, you're as likely to have good luck as bad. I thanked Will and Nick. Their hearts were in the right place.

I rounded the corner to find four people standing outside, Ibraihim amongst them. They all looked nervous, shifting from foot to foot, glancing repeatedly down the street. I waved at them and crossed the street to join them.

They greeted me, but I could tell their attention was directed elsewhere. A sturdy cardboard box sat on the sidewalk, the four of them surrounding it like Emperor penguins guarding an egg. Two of the men, the suicide bomb handlers, I guessed, were dressed in NYPD police uniforms, complete with gun belts, badges and name tags. They'd planned well.

"Is everything okay? You look upset," I said to Ibraihim.

"No, no. Everything is okay," said Ibraihim.

At that moment, a white cargo van rounded the corner and headed our way. Relief flooded their features, seeing it.

The van pulled up in front of the doorway and stopped. The driver stepped out and walked towards Ibraihim.

I took a moment to examine the van. It had a solid side door and solid double rear doors. The only windows were in the driver's compartment. Anyone sitting in back would be unable to see out to the sides and rear. By the same token, nobody could see in.

One of the uniformed terrorists picked up the cardboard box, obviously heavy by the effort it took him, and walked it to the rear of the van.

"Here, allow me to help you," I told him as I moved to open the rear door for him.

"*Shukran.*" Thank you, he said through teeth clenched from strain.

I swung open the rear door and had a look at the interior configuration while he set the box inside. The back was a large, open space that reached forward to a single seat that stretched across the width of the van. The driver's compartment had a driver's seat and passenger seat, with a pass-through between them. 'Economical' is the word that came to mind.

The box loaded, the terrorist backed away and I closed the door, using the move to attach one of the locators to the underside of the bumper. *One down and three to go.* I felt it's magnet click onto the steel.

With the box stowed, the two terrorists climbed quickly into the rear seat and closed the door. The driver got back in, and the fourth man sat in the passenger seat. Doors closed and the van moved away.

The second van rolled up within a minute of the first van's departure. As if on cue, the door to the terrorists' safe house opened and two more terrorists hurried out, also dressed as uniformed NYPD officers. One of them lugged a big box. Once again, I ran to open the rear door for them and looked in. It was identical to the first van, with one difference: the passenger in front was already on board.

The terrorist set the box inside, and I closed the door while attaching a locator under the bumper. *Two down, two to go.* The two uniformed terrorists climbed into the rear seat, the door was closed, and the van left. The New York bombers were on their way.

In less than a minute, the third van pulled up. The safe house door opened and two uniformed terrorists came out, one struggling with a box cradled in his arms. Their uniforms were different from the men going to New York. These mimicked DC Capitol police uniforms, no detail spared.

I moved to open the rear van door, a role I'd successfully assumed, and stepped aside to allow the terrorist to set the box inside, first noting that both the driver and passenger were already on board. Done, I closed the door and attached a locator. *Three down. One to go.* This had been easier than I thought. I reminded myself I wasn't finished yet.

The two uniformed terrorists moved quickly into the rear seat and pulled the door closed behind them. The van pulled out. The first of the DC attackers headed out.

I turned to Ibraihim. "Everything is going well, yes?"

He nodded his head, then turned to watch the approach of the fourth and final van.

It stopped by the door, which opened to allow two more DC Capitol police uniforms to come out. The one carrying the box was Musa, the terrorist who'd confided in me on the walk back from the mosque.

I hurried to open the rear door for him.

As he set the box inside, I glanced forward at the driver's section. Staring back at me from the passenger seat was Stun Gun Man.

He eyed me carefully.

I broke eye contact with him and looked at the driver. Of course. His bodyguard, who else?

I stepped back and closed the rear door while I set the final locator in place. Mission accomplished.

I turned to Musa to wish him well on his journey.

"Thank you, Aiesha." His smile was genuine.

Stun Gun Man climbed out and came around to talk to Ibraihim, his garish neon green and gold shoes shimmering in the afternoon sun. No big deal. Confirming plans, I guessed.

When I saw him glancing back and forth at me and whispering to Ibraihim, my neck hairs leapt to attention. Stun Gun Man had recognized me.

I considered bolting, making a run for it, but it wouldn't change the outcome. They'd only adjust their original plans and strike at different targets, different dates. My best option was to plead innocence, see how it played out.

Ibraihim and Stun Gun Man walked over to me where I stood at the back of the van.

In English, Ibraihim said, "This man claims that he knows you from an earlier encounter," he said, his eyes fixed on mine, challenging.

"My English is not so good. Can we speak in Arabic?" I asked, my eyes directed downward.

"Ajal." Certainly. "To repeat, this man states that he knows you, Aiesha," Ibraihim repeated in Arabic, his voice accusing this time.

"That is not possible. I have never met him," I replied, continuing to play the subordinate while weighing my options.

Stun Gun Man, as it turned out, was not in the mood for an argument. His hand came out of his pants pocket. He held a compact semi-automatic pistol, and he brought it to bear on my wrapped head. "Place your hands behind your back or I will shoot you!" he ordered me.

He stood close enough to me that I could have easily disarmed him and sent him to the hospital, or worse. But what good would that have done? The terror strikes would be called off, and they would all live to fight another day.

I chose to comply, see how things played out.

I placed my hands behind my back and Stun Gun Man zip-tied my wrists together. Then he ordered me to climb into the back of the van. After struggling to get in the back, no easy feat with my hands bound behind me, he zip-tied my ankles together. I was hogtied, unable to move much at all.

Stun Gun Man slammed the door closed, told Ibraihim he would see that I got what I deserved, then got back in the passenger seat.

Musa and his cohort, dressed in their DC Police uniforms, sat on the bench seat in front of me. We drove away from the safe house, on our way to Washington. No one turned to look back at me.

***

It was gloomy in the back of the van where I lay. The only light came from the windshield and the front door windows. The rest of the van was windowless and dark. I laid on my back with the two dirty bombs my only companions.

For starters, I moved to bring my hands under me and out in front, a maneuver I'd practiced many times, and used when Stun Gun Man had left me zip-tied in my apartment. My father first showed me how to do it, and he urged me to maintain my flexibility so I would always be able to do it. Thankfully, I had followed his advice.

I lifted my butt and slid my zip-tied hands downward, then bent my legs so my toes were up against my butt. Then I slid my hands down over my feet and legs. Once I'd cleared my knees, my hands were in front of me.

It took a little longer to get a hand into my pants pocket and extract the small lockback knife I always carry. While working on it, I silently thanked Stun Gun Man for his carelessness in not searching me. I got the knife in my right hand and manipulated it around so I could open the blade with my left. When it locked open, the click it made sounded like a cannon. I lay still a moment, expecting a head or two to turn my way. Nobody paid me any mind.

Relieved, I began the tedious task of cutting through the plastic zip tie binding my wrists. I moved the knife around in my right hand so the blade pointed away from my thumb and the sharp side was towards my wrist. By moving my wrists forward and backward, I produced a sawing motion on the tie. It took some time, because I needed to stretch my wrists apart to keep the zip tie taut, making it easier to cut.

Alternating between sawing the tie and twisting my wrists, I finally cut through enough to break the tie. One down and one to go. Removing the ankle tie proved far easier, but I moved slowly, cautiously, not wanting to attract the attention of my captors.

I didn't have to worry about the driver spotting me in the rearview mirror. I'd seen earlier that there wasn't one. With no rear windows, an inside mirror would have been as useful as a face mask on a fish.

Freed from my bonds, I considered my next move. I had my 3-inch lockback knife, and surprise on my side, my only two weapons. They'd have to do.

Stun Gun Man called out to the two terrorists sitting behind him and asked, "Which one of you wants to be first to go back there and fuck that bitch?"

You just bought yourself a one-way ticket to hell, all expenses paid, asshole!

I waited to see if there were any takers. Musa sat still, but his partner slowly removed his uniform coat and hat and dropped them on the floor beside him. He turned and climbed over the seat, an evil smile working his mouth.

I lay still, my hands tucked under me, knife in hand, pretending to be helpless, for all the world still bound.

The man undid his gun belt and dropped it. Then he stepped out of his trousers and moved in on me, his eyes searching for the best way to take me.

When he grabbed my pants and wrenched them down, I'd had enough.

I brought my right hand out from under me and drove all three inches of my knife blade into his left temple, forward and above his ear. A deep guttural moan escaped from him and he collapsed, unmoving, on top of me.

The guttural moan reached Stun Gun Man's ears. "Put it to her, Abu!" he shouted as I worked my blade out of the dead man's head.

Stun Gun Man lost interest and turned his attention forward.

I shoved the dead terrorist off me and pulled my pants up. Musa sat motionless, staring out through the windshield at the darkening interstate ahead. *Your journey to Paradise will begin sooner than expected, Musa.* I believed he was a man in the wrong place at the wrong time. It was sad, really. Still, I couldn't take the chance that Musa would turn on me. I wiped my knife against the dead terrorist's shirt. I didn't need his slippery blood causing my hand to lose its grip on the handle when I used it on Musa.

Keeping the bulk of my body behind the seat, I reached over the back of it with my left arm and clamped my hand over Musa's mouth, yanking his head backward and into the path of my knife.

I felt the blade sink into the soft tissue below his skull and impact his cervical vertebrae. Moving the blade up, then down, I felt for the cervical space.

Finding it, I slammed the blade forward with the heel of my hand, knowing I needed maximum penetration for my puny blade to reach his spinal column.

His body went limp, signaling to me that I'd succeeded in cutting his spinal cord. His body sagged. All movement ceased. He was dead from the neck down. Without nerves to maintain a beating heart and chest wall movement, his brain would die in seconds.

I pulled him back in the seat, his head lolling lifelessly against the seat back, and worked my blade loose from his neck. Two down. Two to go.

The next man would be a bigger challenge.

Staying low behind the seat, I picked up the first terrorist's gun belt and took the handgun out of its holster. Cradling it in my hand, I knew instantly it wasn't real. A dummy, like the rest of the uniform. I set it quietly on the van floor. Instead, I picked up the uniform jacket.

After removing my *hijab*, I pulled the jacket on and set his Capitol police cap on my head. Holding the knife in my right hand, I eased myself over the seat back and sat down behind Stun Gun Man, who sat on the passenger side, in front. Sensing my presence, he turned halfway around to glance at me, straining to see in the gathering gloom. "How was it, Abu? Think the bitch was a virgin?"

With surprise still in my court, I looped my right hand around his neck and slashed, left to right, deep, with my lockback knife.

There's your one-way ticket to hell, all expenses paid, asshole! I felt the blade cut deep into his exposed neck.

He swung around and came at me with his stun gun, jabbing it at my face as his life blood sprayed out of the gashes that took out both his carotid arteries and bathed the right side of the windshield in crimson.

I clamped my left hand over his stun gun hand and wrenched it sideways, bringing it in contact with Mister Bodyguard, the driver.

Stun Gun Man's hand spasmed, sending nearly four million volts into Mister Bodyguard's shoulder. I strained to keep the stun gun against him, knowing the longer it contacted him the more effective it would be.

When I saw Mister Bodyguard slump sideways and his hands go limp on the steering wheel, I knew he'd had enough. Stun Gun Man began his final journey to hell, his lifeless body collapsing forward against the blood-bathed dash.

With Mister Bodyguard's limp foot weighted down on the accelerator, the van began picking up speed. I glanced through the left side of the windshield, the side not obscured by blood, and saw a bridge abutment rushing at us.

No time to waste.

I squeezed through the space between the front seats, unfastening the driver's seat belt as I made my way into the space. My head scraped the roof, and the police cap was knocked from my head.

I gripped the wheel with my right hand, keeping the van on a straight course down the interstate, and reached across the front of the driver with my left hand. I yanked the door handle up and shoved the driver's inert body towards the door.

We were screaming down the highway at better than eighty miles an hour, and the wind resistance on the door made it nearly impossible to push open. Nearly.

With all the strength I could muster, I heaved my hips and upper body against the driver's bulk. Gradually, I forced the door open with the driver's body and propelled him out onto the roadway. A screeching of brakes immediately followed. I focused on the task of steering the van away from the bridge abutment and bringing it to a stop in the breakdown lane.

With the van at a complete stop, I threw the shift lever into Park and drew a deep breath, beginning to blow off the abundance of adrenaline coursing through my veins.

I quickly became aware of a vehicle screeching to a stop next to me. I turned to see two rifles aimed at me and my side of the van. Then I heard someone shout, "Don't shoot! That's EZ!" The rifles were lowered.

Doors opened and two men in SWAT gear raced at me. One yanked open my door, the other did the same with the side door.

"Step out!" the man at my door commanded.

I stepped down, relief flooding through my mind. Seeing me, his face filled with concern. "You hurt, Miss?"

"I'm good," I replied, locking my eyes with his.

He stared at my face, my arms.

I looked down, and immediately knew the reason for his concern. I wore the DC coat of the terrorist, which was drenched in blood sprayed on me by Stun Gun Man, and likely from the other two terrorists as well. "That's not my blood," I explained.

While he looked me over, the second agent climbed in the back of the van and checked the two terrorists for signs of life, then came forward to check Stun Gun Man. Finished, he turned to me and said, "You did all this by yourself." It could have been a question, but he made it a statement.

I nodded to him in the affirmative. "I had no choice. Either me or them."

"Nice fuckin' goin'!" he remarked, looking me in the eye, clearly impressed.

"Thanks."

While two agents hefted the lifeless body of the driver and dropped it behind the rear seat, a third agent opened the rear door and checked out the box containing the dirty bombs. He picked it up and carried it to the rear of the SUV, then carefully transferred each device into what looked like an oversized cooler. I watched as he lifted them out one by one, saw they were designed to look like a construction cone, right down to their fluorescent orange paint. A policeman carrying a construction cone. No threat there, to the average observer. Clever, I had to admit.

The agent handling them added padding around them, then closed the cover and fastened it with side clamps.

"What's that box you stowed them in?" I asked, watching.

"It's a lead-lined container designed to block any radiation. The terrorists didn't use any shielding, probably because of the added weight, so there's a lot of radiation leaking out," he explained.

I told him about the woman's symptoms back at the safe house.

"Yeah, sounds like radiation poisoning to me," he concurred.

"So, what's happening with the other three vans?" I asked, curious.

The leader spoke up. "The other three pursuit vehicles are in position behind the vans, waiting for full darkness and a break in traffic before they attack. We hadn't planned on intercepting your van until we saw it picking up speed and driving erratically. Fortunately, it happened with few other vehicles around."

"And even more fortunate, you didn't shoot first and ask questions later," I commented drily.

"That, too," he conceded. "I'll call Agent Yukon and give him an update. He'll be glad to hear you're okay," he added with a nod in my direction. He took out his cell phone and hit a speed dial number, then spoke softly.

After a time, he turned to me, holding out his phone. "He wants a word with you, EZ."

I took the phone. "Hey, boss. Everything's good."

He asked for my version of the takedown. I relived it all. He listened without interruption. "You continue to impress me, EZ, and that's hard to do."

"I appreciate that, sir."

"We may need you back here in Miami. One of the agents will drive the van back so forensics can go over it, make sure we didn't miss anything. You take his seat in the SUV, they'll bring you back to the stakeout, okay?"

"Works for me, sir. I've seen more than enough of the men in the van," I said.

"I'm sure. Call me when you're situated."

I handed the phone back to the agent in charge. He took it from me and said, "Hop aboard, EZ. Agent Tully gets the honor of driving the meat wagon to Miramar." Miramar was FBI headquarters.

Before we left, I took off the Capitol police jacket and threw it into the van, then retrieved my discarded hijab, pleased to see it had escaped the gore. I reached for my folding knife I'd dropped on the front floor mat, but the agent stopped me. "Sorry, that stays. Evidence. I'll see you get it back after. Promise."

I thanked him and climbed into the passenger seat. We reversed directions, the van following us, and headed back to Miami.

With most of the adrenaline gone from my system, fatigue took over. I partially reclined my seat, leaned back and closed my eyes for a moment, intending to give them a short rest.

Next I knew, the driver was telling me we were back.

I peered out my window to see the door to the stakeout building. Checked the dash clock, and saw it was nearly ten. Time flies when you're having fun.

I thanked the driver, looked both ways to be sure nobody was out there, and stepped down to the empty street. The bomb agent came around and took my seat and the SUV drove off.

I ducked inside and climbed the stairs. Jack met me, gun held at the ready. Seeing me, he relaxed, and put the gun away.

"Welcome back, EZ. Heard you had a hell of a time. By the looks of you, it's all true."

I guessed he was referring to the coat of blood I was wearing.

"Word travels fast," I replied, smiling at him.

"When Will and Nick saw them hogtie you and throw you in the back of the van, they called Agent Yukon for instructions. He told them to stay out of it, you could take care of yourself and that he'd make sure the agents didn't shoot you. Guess you handled it," he added, grinning at me.

"Yup. So, what's going on across the street?" I asked, moving the attention away from me.

"They're down to a skeleton crew. That guy, Ibraihim, one other guy, and a couple women, near as we can tell. Looks like they're hanging out, waiting for the last boat to come in," he surmised.

"Any visitors since I left?"

"Nope. It's been really boring," Alberto commented.

"Anybody got any water? I'm dry as a bone," I said.

Alberto spoke up. "There's a bottle of water and a sub in the fridge. Agent Yukon told me to get it for you, for when you showed up. Man's got a lot of foresight," he added, glancing at me. Then he pointed at my face. "You may want to wash up before you eat."

My sudden thirst had pushed thoughts of the blood spatter from my mind. "Good idea," I said, then stepped into the bathroom.

Although the blood had dried to a dull black color, it still made a mess of my face and hands. I stripped off the hijab and parahaan, and stood before the mirror in my bra. Someone had left a hand towel.

I turned on the water and began wetting the towel, wiping away the cloying bloodstains. When I'd finished, I took another minute to rinse out the sink. It looked like it had been in a fight of its own, came out second.

I let my body air dry a moment, then pulled the parahaan over my head. I left the hijab off. It felt good to be clean, but even better not being confined by the head scarf. I turned off the light and left the bathroom.

Alberto had set my bottle of water on the table with a bag of corn chips and a sandwich. The water got my attention first. I hadn't realized how thirsty I'd become. I picked it up, spun the cap off, and sipped half of it.

Seeing me cleaned up, Alberto laughed. "You look a whole lot better, EZ. Glad to have you back."

I took his comment to mean 'glad you're back safely from the mess you've been through' as well as 'glad to have you back to your regular routine.' I thanked him, getting it.

I pulled a chair up to the table and ate the sandwich and chips. Even though the sandwich was a little mushy, I thought it tasted wonderful at nine-thirty. It felt damned good to be alive, unharmed. Thinking back on the van ordeal, I knew the outcome could have gone in a completely different direction. Things had worked in my favor, is all.

Finished, I balled up the paper and took my shot. It hit the waste basket rim, teetered there on the rim for a moment, then rolled in. Kind of like how my evening had gone. In the end, everything worked out. Dad would say I planned well. Lady luck had stayed out of it.

I put on the headset to review the conversations recorded after I'd left. Silence dominated much of it, allowing me to fast-forward through it.

I caught a conversation, Ibraihim speaking to Fatimah.

"How could I have been so stupid as to trust that Aiesha woman?" he asked Fatimah.

Her answer surprised me.

"How can you be sure that she truly was a traitor? Perhaps he said that to you because he wanted to take her along, have his way with her on the journey to Washington. She is, after all, a beautiful young woman," Fatimah offered.

"You are right, darling. I may have acted in haste, allowing him to take her. We may never know the truth."

I smiled, hearing this. I had Fatimah in my court.

Ibraihim concluded the conversation by saying that their work was nearly complete. "In a few hours, the final boat will arrive, and by tomorrow afternoon they will have carried out their mission. Then we can go back to our normal, anonymous lives."

Fat chance, Ibraihim. You're miles beyond that.

I listened to the rest of the tape, fast-forwarding through the silence, until I'd scanned it all. Alberto was right. No visitors, nothing unusual. Trust but verify, I always say.

I looked at Jack. "Any idea what Agent Yukon plans to do about the third boatload of terrorists?"

"He'd only say he has it covered, wouldn't go into detail," Jack answered. "Guess it's above our pay grade," he added, keeping his eyes on the safe house.

"I'll see if I can find anything out," I replied, punching in the number on my phone.

Yukon answered quickly. He'd had a busy day, and it looked like it would be a long night.

"I'm back, sir. Everything's quiet here. You need me to go to my boat, do anything?"

"For now, no. We don't want to run the risk of alerting the bad guys, so we're keeping our distance. I got things covered. Things change, you'll be the first to know," he said.

"Thanks, sir. I'll watch and wait here, then."

"Perfect," he replied, and clicked off.

I set my phone down.

"Look!" Jack said, and pointed out the window.

I saw a black sedan pull up and stop. Out stepped Lieutenant Lopez, highlighted by the street light nearby. looking for all the world that he owned the street, or at least that part of it. He walked briskly to the safe house door and knocked. After a brief pause, it opened.

The light inside illuminated the figure of Ibraihim. He stepped back and Lopez entered. Then the door closed on them.

What are you doing, Lopez?

I put the headset on and tried to hear something, anything, that would shed light on why Lopez had become a frequent visitor.

At first the voices were muffled, distant, though I could hear shouting, arguing between the two. Then the volume of their voices increased and I could pick up a word or two, but it wasn't making any sense.

They must have walked down the corridor to the living area, because their voices got clearer. Lopez was arguing, pleading, maybe. Then his words became distinct. "So after they come ashore tonight, we're even, right? You'll give me the evidence and we'll go our separate ways."

"That's the deal, Lieutenant. You got my word," said Ibraihim.

"I can't believe I let myself get involved with you in the first place," Lopez complained, his voice rising.

"You let your other head take control of you, is all. Could happen to any man," Ibraihim replied, his voice full of smug amusement.

"So when I escort them here tonight, you'll turn over the evidence to me?"

"I've already told you. Yes. It's the last thing you need to do for me," Ibraihim explained patiently.

"All right. I'll wait at the dock and see everyone gets here safely. Then we're done," said Lopez firmly.

"Then we're done," confirmed Ibraihim.

"I'll let myself out."

A moment later the door opened and Lopez emerged. He moved swiftly to his cruiser, climbed in and drove off.

"That was interesting," I said in a soft voice.

"What?" asked Jack, who heard my comment.

I explained what I'd heard.

"Yep, that's interesting."

I called Yukon to fill him in. After I summarized the conversation I'd heard, he told me not to do anything.

"I don't know what they have on Lopez, but whatever it is, it's not going to affect the outcome."

He told me that the second van going to DC had been taken down. "All occupants were neutralized and the devices remained intact."

"Two down and two to go," I said, impressed. Then Yukon corrected me.

"No. Two down and *three* to go."

I started to ask him for more detail, but he'd already disconnected. Clearly, he had a plan to take down the third boatload of terrorists and their bombs, rendezvousing at two O'clock, but was playing it close to the hip.

I told Jack and Alberto the second van had been taken down without incident, and they high-fived me, grinning. I told them Yukon wanted Lopez left to his own devices. They nodded in agreement.

We settled into our routine, a half hour of watching, an hour of rest. Time crawled slowly by. Ten. Eleven. Midnight. One. No traffic. No visitors. Though I knew I needed sleep, I also knew I wouldn't be getting any. There was too much excitement in the air.

Shortly after two, we all heard what sounded like a clap of thunder. We glanced at each other, wondering what we'd heard. The weather was clear, with no forecast for storms. We listened intently, but heard nothing further. Puzzled, we went back to watching and waiting.

Twenty minutes later my cell phone went off. Seeing it was Yukon, I answered it.

"Five down, none to go," he announced in a calm, matter-of-fact voice.

"Tell me."

He said that the other two vans had been neutralized. The third one had overturned after being shot up, but the bombs didn't detonate and remained intact. The fourth and final van had slowed and nearly came to a stop on its own, the driver taken out, but it hit a bridge abutment, a glancing blow, before it stopped.

"You know those orange barrels they put around the bridge abutments to slow vehicles down? It plowed into a couple of them, losing a lot of speed, before it whacked the abutment. Good news is, the bombs stayed intact through it all. We recovered all four of them," Yukon told me, satisfaction in his voice.

"That's wonderful!" I said, giving the guys a thumbs up. I'd explain to them later what happened. "What about the boat?"

"Did you hear or feel an explosion a half hour ago?"

"We did. It sounded like a clap of thunder to us."

"It was a Hellfire missile, exploding a hundred feet above the two boats. We tracked the pickup boat with a drone. When the drone's infrared camera showed the two boats converging below, we passed the coordinates on to an F-35 flying above. The drone provided laser guidance for the Hellfire. After the missile detonated, we had a SEAL team move in to assess damage and neutralize any survivors."

"Wow, that's intense," I said.

"They found the two boats ablaze, destroyed nearly to their waterlines. Surprisingly, they found the telltale suitcase in the hull of one of the boats. It had received minor damage, but it remained intact enough for the SEALS to fish it out and transport it back. There were no survivors. They counted eight bodies, which was the number we figured on. The SEALS sank what was left of the two boats, the eight bodies included. Mission accomplished," Yukon summarized with satisfaction.

"That's great," I said, impressed.

"Last, but not least, I've got a strike team on the way to take down the remaining residents of the safe house. I'm guessing you and the two agents there want to be part of the entry."

"Damn right we do!"

"I thought as much. I've instructed the team leader to expect you. I've briefed him about you. Meet them outside your doorway. They should be there any time."

"Thank you, sir!" True to form, he'd already disconnected.

I quickly filled Jack and Alberto in on the Hellfire missile strike's success, as well as what was going down at the safe house. We hurried from the room and down the stairs to the street entrance. We pushed open the door and found the strike team members waiting for us.

The team leader looked at me. "EZ, right? I'm Zack."

"Yes, I'm EZ," I confirmed.

"You're the only one who has been inside the safe house. Tell me the layout."

I gave him all the details I could, explaining that I hadn't been through all the rooms in the building.

"It's a start. Thanks. Let's roll!" he said in a voice loud enough for all to hear.

We moved as one around the corner and up to the safe house door. Two men with an entry ram moved forward and, in a coordinated move, rammed the door by the lockset. The door exploded inward, the jamb shattered, and two men rushed past them and inside, M4 assault rifles held at the ready. The rest of the team followed, with the two agents and me taking up the rear.

"What is the meaning of this?" I heard Ibraihim shout, trying to sound indignant.

"Where are the others?" shouted Zack, the team leader, ignoring Ibraihim's question.

"I am alone here, with my wife and another woman," he replied.

"Where are they?" Zack demanded.

"They are in that room," Ibraihim said, pointing at the door to the room where I'd been searched.

Three agents moved to the door. One swung it open and the other two rushed inside, guns at the ready. In short order they reemerged, with Fatimah and another woman escorted by the agents. Seeing her, I moved forward. Her eyes widened in surprise as she recognized me.

"Aiesha, is it you?" she whispered.

"Yes, it is," I whispered back.

"But I saw you taken away by that cruel man. I thought he meant to kill you."

"It's a long story, Fatimah, for another time. For now, I want to see that you get treated for radiation sickness. I will do what I can to help you through this."

Zack ordered his men to search the rest of the building, and four men fanned out. With congestion considerably reduced, Ibraihim glanced our way and recognized me.

His mouth gaped. "You! How is this possible?"

"Anything's possible, Ibraihim. Right now, I want the evidence you have on Lieutenant Lopez." I held his eyes with mine, something he hadn't experienced when I presented myself to him as Aiesha.

"I don't know what you're talking about," he insisted, putting on a stern face.

"Save your breath. We have your conversation with Lopez on tape."

The realization of how much trouble he was in finally hit him, and he collapsed into one of the chairs. "It is hidden under the mattress in there," he told me, pointing at the room the women had come from. An agent hurried into the room and tossed the mattress.

"Got it!" he called out, then returned with a manila envelope in his hands. He held it out to me, but Zack intervened.

"Evidence," he informed me, taking it from the agent.

"Can I have a look at it? I've had dealings with Lieutenant Lopez and I'm curious how he's being blackmailed," I told Zack.

"Since Yukon gave you top marks, yeah, go ahead," he said, handing the envelope to me. "I'll look over your shoulder to make sure it all goes back in the envelope," he added.

I took it from him and opened the flap, sliding the contents into my hand. Six photographs. All 8 x 10 glossies. Each showed Lieutenant Lopez having sex with an attractive young Arab woman. Same bed, different positions. The identical date and time printed on the bottom of each one, a good six months earlier than my first encounter with Lopez.

I slid the photos back in the envelope and handed it back to Zack, the pieces falling into place. Lopez got lured into having sex with a woman that wasn't his wife. Photos were taken of him, then showed to him. That got his attention. The blackmailer, Ibraihim I guessed, asked him to do certain things so the photos wouldn't get sent to his wife. Three of the things he was asked to do involved passing messages on from six incarcerated individuals caught trying to rob the safe at the Adriatic Hotel. Lopez would have considered it a small price to pay to keep his wife out of the loop.

When it all shook down, I guessed internal affairs would be given the photos and do their investigation of Lopez. I doubted that Mrs. Lopez would stick with him. I wondered if Lopez knew how close his city had come to being the victim of a dirty nuclear bomb attack.

With a suddenness that surprised me, I realized how exhausted I was. Things were under control in the safe house, and I knew I'd have to give my statement, but hoped it could wait until tomorrow. I asked Zack.

"Don't know why not. Check it out with Yukon, okay?"

Typical example of CYA: cover your ass.

I told him okay, and speed-dialed Yukon. I filled him in on the safe house raid, mentioned the photos of Lopez, and gave him my version of what likely happened.

"Go get some sleep, EZ. You've earned it. Come by in the morning." He signed off before I could say 'yes, sir.'

I told Zack everything was cool, and I left the safe house. My little red Fiat carried me to my apartment, and I was having a look at the backsides of my eyelids in no time.

***

In the morning over coffee, I watched a news broadcast on TV about a mysterious sonic boom that occurred out over the Atlantic late last night. The report was vague, and no eyewitness accounts could shed any additional light.

Following that, I went to my laptop and did a search for accidents or events along the I-95 corridor in the past twelve hours. Two reports jumped out at me.

The first was called in by a driver who passed a white van that had impacted a bridge abutment, but he was waved on by two official-looking men when he slowed to see if he could help.

The second was called in by another driver. He came upon a white van that had overturned on the roadside, and he, too, was waved on by two official-looking men at the scene.

In both incidents, when police arrived at the scenes to investigate, they found nothing. The report went on to say that the police suspected the same man of calling in both false reports.

The FBI guys had been thorough.

***

I packed up my meager belongings, figuring my time in this fancy apartment had run out, and drove to the Miramar FBI building. I parked and walked in like I owned the place. Guess I owned a piece of it since I pay my taxes. I found Agent Yukon's office in the maze and tapped on the door.

"Come in," came his voice from within.

I opened the door and stepped inside.

He looked up from the pile of papers on his desk. "EZ, sit." He maintained his reputation of a man of few words.

I sat in the chair opposite him.

"I have to admit it, Miss Kelly. Your work has been impressive," he announced as, palms on his desk, he eased himself back in his chair.

"Aw, shucks, sir. It was nothing," I countered, doing a lousy Gomer Pyle imitation.

"You know better. Hold on a sec." He picked up his desk phone, hit a button, and after a pause said, "She's here," then replaced the receiver. The mysterious Agent Yukon. He turned his attention back to me.

"So, as of now, our contract with you is up, and your new position behind the tour desk at the Adriatic is waiting for you, starting the first of the week. That is, unless you'd like to come to work with us," he dangled out there.

"I've had enough excitement to hold me for a while, sir. I'll keep your offer in mind, but for now I'm ready to go back to the Adriatic Monday morning," I replied, thinking how good it sounded.

"I figured you would be. I'll need your car and apartment keys, plus your set of fake IDs. Keep the clothes, for what they're worth," he added.

"So I get to keep the boat?"

"Nice try. I'll need that key, too."

"Can't blame me for trying."

I took the keys and IDs from my purse and spread them on the desk in front of me. At the same time, there came a knock at the door.

"Come in," barked Yukon.

The door swung wide and Agent Brophy stepped in, grinning from ear to ear as he grabbed me and gave me a big hug. I hugged him back.

When we separated, he said, "You're looking good, EZ."

"You are, too, Rick. Where's your cane?"

"I ditched it. Still a little gimpy, but I'm better every day," he told me, a big smile spreading across his face.

"That's great! Can't keep a good man down, right?"

"Something like that. Spoken to your old man recently?"

"Not recently. I've got to call him, let him know I'm all right," I said.

"Let's call him together," suggested Brophy. I haven't talked to the old buzzard in some time, and that'll give me the chance to tell him myself that he raised one hell of a daughter."

"Sounds like a plan, Rick."

Yukon spoke up. "You know, EZ, this whole deal never happened. Make sure you keep your comments to broad generalities. Your dad's been there. He'll understand."

"Of course," I said, nodding.

"Okay. Couple more things," he said, reaching in his desk drawer. "Here's the keys for your Beetle and your apartment." He slid my key ring across to me. "I've taken the liberty to direct-deposit your salary and bonus into your checking account."

"I don't recall giving you my bank information," I responded.

"It wasn't hard to locate," he replied, sweeping a hand over his balding head.

His hand went back into his desk drawer and withdrew something. "After all it's done for you, I think you should have this back, too." He held out his hand.

Resting in it was my lockback knife that had helped me raise hell inside the van. Someone did a good job cleaning it up. I accepted it, hefted it, and dropped it in my pocket.

"Thank you. That little guy has been with me a long time," I said, genuinely smiling at him.

"Can you think of anything we've missed?" he asked.

"No, sir. Thanks for all the back-up. Couldn't have done the mission without it," I told him with all sincerity.

"It cuts both ways, EZ."

"We done here?" asked Rick, eyes on Agent Yukon.

"I'd say so," Yukon replied.

"Cause if we are, EZ and I are going out for lunch together," Rick said. "Right, EZ?"

"No argument from me," I said, smiling at both of them.

I finger-saluted Yukon and he returned the salute, all business. Agent Rick Brophy linked his arm in mine and escorted me out the door, and out through the main entrance of the FBI building. The noonday sun felt soothing, comforting on my upturned face.

As we made our way to his car, I heard a car door open. On instinct I turned towards it, my senses still on alert. Seeing a man standing there, I sucked in a surprised breath.

"Dad! How'd you get here?" I cried as I rushed to him, arms

outstretched. He surrounded me in his strong arms and hugged me close.

With the initial surge of emotion dissipating, I leaned back and examined his war-scarred face.

He grinned at me, his eyes squinting in the late morning sunshine. "That old fart you're with called me last night, said today was a good time to come see you," Dad explained. "Your mom and I got a flight out, and here we are."

As he spoke, I watched the passenger door open and Mom stepped out.

"Oh my God! Mom!" I called as I raced around the car to collect her in my arms. Remembering her severe arthritis, I went easy with my hug. I was surprised when she hugged me fiercely.

I returned the hug, then looked her in the eye. "Are you feeling better, Mom?" I asked, remembering the pain I'd seen on her face.

"I am, EZ. I'm on a new medicine. Injections once a month, and it's given me a lot of my mobility back," she explained.

"Oh, that's wonderful!" I said, hugging her anew.

Looking over Mom's shoulder, I watched as Dad and Rick got reacquainted. The two men bro-hugged each other. Two old warriors coming together again with shared memories, some good, some bad, drawing them together like magnets. After what I'd gone through, I knew how they felt.

At length they separated, slapped each other on their backs and struggled to regain their composure. My heart swelled with pride when I heard Rick tell Dad that he'd raised one hell of a daughter. I'd heard him say it before, but hearing it said directly to Dad was special.

Rick turned to Mom and me and said, "Let's get out of here. I've got a reservation all set at a good restaurant. It'd be a shame to have them cancel it."

He led the way to his car, Dad at his side, Mom and I following close behind. Rick and Dad got in the front and Mom and I climbed in the back seat. She and I made small talk and held each other's hands while Rick drove us to the restaurant. I lost track of where we were going, immersed as I was in getting caught up with Mom. She told me my brother—I still called him Junior—now a Navy Seal, was stationed at the Pensacola Naval Air Station here in Florida. So near and yet so far.

When Rick turned the car off, I looked out the side window to see we were at one of the classier establishments in Miami. Definitely a cut above my pay grade. Rick continued to surprise me.

We clambered out of the car and headed into the restaurant. Inside, Rick approached the maître d'. "Brophy, table for five."

While the maître d' checked his reservation sheet, I glanced around, confused. There were four of us: Rick, Dad, Mom and me. Why had Rick said *five*? I guessed he was a little flustered.

The maître d' beckoned us to follow and led the way into the restaurant to a table already occupied by a soldier dressed in full uniform, his back to us.

Seeing Rick and Dad, the soldier got carefully to his feet.

Recognition washed over me, leaving me weak, clinging to Mom for support. *Paul.*

He turned to me with a warm smile, reaching out to me. He stepped towards me, arms wide.

I let go of Mom and rushed into his embrace, our bodies fitting together as if they'd never been apart.

"I love you, EZ," he whispered in my ear.

"Ditto, kiddo," I whispered back, the expression I'd used with him light years ago.

He pulled back far enough to plant a warm kiss on my lips.

"Enough already!" said Rick. "Introduce me to this young man."

I did so, and I watched Paul and Rick exchange words and handshakes. But something about how Paul moved set alarm bells off in my head.

"Are you okay, Paul?" I asked, sensing something wrong.

"Sit! Sit!" commanded Rick, and we all obeyed.

I made sure I had the seat next to Paul, and watched him gingerly lower himself onto his chair.

"What is it?" I asked him in a whisper, afraid of what he might say.

Despite my whisper, everyone else was alerted by my question. Everyone looked to Paul for an answer.

"I've been at Reed the past six weeks," he began. We all knew Reed was Walter Reed Army Medical Center in Washington, DC. We waited for Paul to continue.

"I got burns from a poorly-improvised explosive device. We nickname them PIEDs, instead of straight IEDs. Lucky for me, it was poorly improvised."

When I heard "lucky" I glanced at Dad, who raised his brows and shook his head. I knew what he was thinking. I turned back to Paul.

"Instead of an explosion, the device created an intense hot flash. I had my back to it, which saved me. My backpack and helmet shielded my upper body, but my butt and the backs of my legs got cooked. After initial treatment at the field hospital in Afghanistan, they shipped me to Germany, and then on to Reed."

He turned to me and whispered, "Remember my heart tattoo?"

I knew what he meant. He'd gotten a red heart with my initials on it tattooed on his right shoulder before he shipped out.

"Of course I do," I said.

"It's now on my butt. They used it as a graft," he said, chuckling.

With the mental image in my head, I laughed out loud.

"What're you two whispering about? You want to share?" said Rick.

"Nope. It's personal, Rick," I cryptically replied, still laughing.

He ignored me. "So how much longer at Reed?"

Paul said he had another three or four more weeks of treatment to go. "It's still touchy to sit, especially on hard chairs," he said. "But it beats the hell out of lying on my chest all the time."

"How'd you get here?" I asked, still surprised to see him.

"The doc came in my room late last night and told me I had a 48-hour pass to go to Miami. He handed me a round trip airline ticket and told me to get my shit, I mean my stuff, together. My beneficiary's right there," he said, pointing to Dad.

All eyes turned to Dad.

"Hey, I thought it wouldn't be a proper get-together without Paul. I called his dad and found out he was at Reed, so I contacted them. They told me he was well enough for a short furlough. I made the arrangements."

I looked at Dad and my vision blurred for a moment as tears welled up. "I love you, Dad." It was all I could say.

"I love you, too, EZ girl!" Then he rolled his head to the side. "Just kidding! You're no girl. By the way, I'd've had Junior here, too, but he's involved in a debriefing. Seems his team jumped into the Atlantic off the Florida coast last night, who knows why?"

His words hit home. He'd just told me Junior was part of the Seal Team that cleaned up the mess left by the Hellfire missile. It was good knowing he was safe.

In less than an hour, my world had shrunk to a table for five in a classy Miami restaurant. I sat there, basking in the sheer joy of it and squeezed Paul's hand to make sure he was real.

Dear Reader,

If you enjoyed *Easy Kill*, be on the lookout for the next book in the EZ Kelly series. *Easy Save*, book 2, is under construction. There is no question that a part of me and what life has taught me has been passed along into *Easy Kill*. I love military stories—everything from *The Red Badge of Courage, All Quiet on the Western Front, From Here to Eternity*, down to *Audie Murphy the Soldier*, Stephen Hunter's Bob Lee Swagger series, and Navy SEAL Chris Kyle's *American Sniper*, and so many more.

I certainly cannot fail to mention Lee Child's Jack Reacher series, since my lead character, EZ Kelly, was conceived by me as a who could be Jack Reacher's counterpart. *Easy Kill* is the first novel of my series and her career as a travel agent will carry her far and wide on future adventures.

An excerpt from my next novel, *Easy Save*, follows. I hope you find it entertaining. I promise to get the whole story to you soon.

—Charles M. DuPuy
February, 2018

Excerpt from *Easy Save*

I watched the young couple huddle over the rack of tour brochures. I kept their images in my peripheral vision while doing my best to appear busy. The guy looked eighteen, the girl was maybe fourteen. Statutory rape came to mind.

The young man stood tall and lean, with light brown hair cut short. He had a blond beard that barely showed. His narrow face sported a long, narrow nose perched above a thin mouth. He looked energetic, robust, ready for what life brought him. Turned out, he'd need every bit of that.

I guessed the girl's height at around five-six, with a slim but shapely figure and corn silk blonde hair held in a ponytail. She had an oval face with blue eyes and lips most women would die for. Clearly, she'd draw stares wherever she went, despite her youth.

Most of the people drawn to my rack of Florida tour brochures are lookers, passing time glancing at the multi-colored pictures, their brains in neutral, nothing registering. That's maybe ninety percent of them. Sort of like people who stroll down the street and eyeball shop windows, nothing on their mind, nothing on their shopping list. The other ten percent are what I call tire kickers. Like the people who go to car dealerships and ask endless questions about the different models, tying up the salesman's time, then end up giving the tire a kick on their way out, no plans to return, no plans to buy.

The guy plucked out a brochure and the two of them, heads together, examined it like Darwin eyeballing a new species. After a short exchange, they turned and approached my desk, smiling. At the same time, I noticed a thirtyish-looking woman standing behind them at the brochure rack. Maybe it would be a good day for me.

The young man glanced at the nameplate on my desk, shifted his gaze upwards to me, a quizzical expression overspreading his brow. "E? or do I say E Z?" he asked.

My nameplate says I'm EZ Kelly. Confuses a lot of people. "Call me EZ. Everyone does," I replied, smiling at him.

"Ah, of course!" he said, getting it. "Anyway, Melissa and I think the Everglades tour sounds cool. What can you tell us about it?"

"It so happens that I'm going on that tour tomorrow," I said. "It's my day off, and every week I go on a different tour so I can tell my customers first-hand what to expect. I agree with you, it sounds like a blast. Ever been on an airboat?"

"No, I, we, never have," he said, speaking for both of them.

"You'll love it. It's like riding in an open boat powered by an airplane engine. A little noisy, but you fly over the water. Then they'll slow down enough so you can see alligators and manatees, maybe snakes and turtles, plus a whole raft of tropical birds along the way." I grinned for good measure.

"The bus picks you up here at the hotel and takes you to Everglades City where you board an airboat for the wild trip through the Everglades. Your guide will point out the wildlife as you go along. After the ride, you'll go to one of Everglade City's great restaurants for lunch. If you're the adventurous type, you can try alligator served many different ways. After lunch, you can walk around the exhibits and stores. The buses load up again at three for the return trip. You should be back here at the Adriatic Hotel by around four. How does all that sound?"

Watching the youthful enthusiasm on their faces, I could tell I'd made a sale.

"It sounds perfect!" the young man gushed.

"Yeah, way cool!" agreed the girl, smiling up at him.

"Okay, when do you want to go?"

"Will tomorrow work?" he asked, his eyebrows raised in anticipation.

"Let me check." I picked up my phone and punched in the familiar number. Meanwhile, the thirtyish-looking woman, brochure in hand, had taken up a position behind the two of them, clearly within earshot.

Waiting for my call to be answered, I asked, "Where are you folks from?"

"Columbia, South Carolina," said the handsome young spokesman. "I'm Ted and this is Melissa. We're siblings," he added.

I guessed that wasn't the first time he'd clarified the situation.

"Nice to meet you both." I reached out and shook their hands. Both offered firm handshakes. "You already know my name. I'm EZ Kelly," I confirmed.

At that moment my call was answered, helping to mask my surprise. I'd assumed they were young lovers, not close-knit siblings. No statutory rape there.

I confirmed that they could join tomorrow's tour, and the two of them whooped and high-fived at the news. Then I had them sit while I got the information needed to complete the forms and collect their money.

While doing so, I learned a little more about them. Ted had graduated from high school and enlisted in the army. His parents wanted the two of them to take a trip together so they'd have shared memories. Nice parents.

"I spent time in the army, Ted. Hope your time is enjoyable."

"Oh, yeah? What branch?" he asked, curious.

"Special Forces," I replied, smiling, making light of it.

"No kidding, that's awesome! That's what *I* want to do!" His enthusiasm was infectious.

"Good luck with that. I think you have what it takes."

Ted's face reddened slightly with the compliment. "Thanks," he responded, his eyes holding mine.

I finished up, took their money.

"Be here by eight tomorrow morning to meet the bus. Hope that isn't a problem," I added, thinking how teenagers liked to sleep in.

"No problem. We'll be here in plenty of time."

"Oh, and bring sunscreen," I said. "It's likely to get hot out there on the airboat in June, and with the wind in your hair you won't notice how intense it is."

"Thanks for the tip, Miss Kelly. See you at eight tomorrow morning," said Ted.

"No problem. And call me EZ. Calling me Miss Kelly makes me feel like an old woman."

"You're far from that," he said, giving me a warm smile.

"Thanks. I hope my being along on the tour doesn't take the fun out of it for you and Melissa."

"Are you kidding? You being along won't change a thing. Everything'll be fine," he replied, smiling broadly.

After a final thanks, they bounded off for parts unknown, and the woman behind them stepped forward. She had severe features over what had likely been a pleasant, youthful face. She looked strong.

I stood to greet her, extended my hand.

"Hi. I'm EZ Kelly. How may I help you?"

She gave my hand a limp shake.

Ugh.

"I couldn't help overhearing about the Everglades trip. It sounds like fun. Is this the tour?" she asked, holding up the brochure in her hand for me to see.

I glanced at it, confirmed that it was.

"Thank you. I'm going to show it to my husband. He's not much of a tourist, but I think he'll enjoy it. I'll get back to you if he does," she told me, the attempt at a smile working on her face.

"Sure," I replied, smiling back at her.

The woman moved away from me and sat in one of the lobby's upholstered chairs, then took out her cell phone and punched in a number. When her call was answered, she spoke slowly, quietly, carefully.

"I've found a good one. Fourteen, maybe fifteen, blonde, going on an Everglades trip with her brother." She recited the tour information from the brochure she held, then listened.

"Yes, tomorrow. Short notice, I know, but well worth it. The wheel chair and black wig should work fine," she added, then closed her phone.

Acknowledgements

I wish to express my appreciation for the encouragement and support given to me by my many Facebook friends, especially to JW Wood and DA Kori Prier, whose suggestions and encouragement have helped to move my writing career forward.

In addition, I extend my heartfelt thanks to my publisher, Brittiany Koren at Written Dreams Publishing who took on the challenge of transforming my manuscript into a living, breathing and polished novel.

My thanks also go out to my many friends and relatives who have followed me and my stories as I moved along the path towards becoming a published author. Their quiet support, enthusiasm and optimism has helped to carry me through many tough times, and pushed me forward as I polished my craft.

Last, but not least by any means, thank you, Janet for your quiet support and encouragement, and for your tolerance of my long sessions spent with my computer, without which I could have easily abandoned my quest.

Parts Unknown

An Alaskan Mystery

Toni Niesen

Somewhere over the Alaskan wilderness a plane has disappeared.

As winter approaches Anchorage, flight instructor Beri Quinn races to find a student who took off in one of her planes, and hasn't been seen since. She's convinced he's still alive despite the Civil Air Patrol calling off their search. She strives to locate the missing pilot, save her reputation as a flight instructor and keep her business. But both in the air and on land, she must overcome gathering forces conspiring against her.

A single mother, Quinn fears losing custody of her son. She draws on her knowledge of aviation and musters the emotional strength necessary to overcome unseen adversaries and protect her family. With missing gold, sabotaged aircraft and unsolved murder, the stakes are high for Quinn and for her enemies.

To resolve her dilemma, Beri must answer one underlying question: did her student misjudge the weather and make a fatal mistake, or was he the victim of an elaborate murder plot? In her quest for an answer, she discovers unexpected betrayal and a massive criminal conspiracy.

Told with suspense, humor, and a fighting spirit, this is a mystery for anyone who has ever dreamed of adventure in Alaska.

VO2 Max

Book 3 of the Tri-Angles Series

Katharine M. Nohr

Can Zana West help new pro-triathletes stay on the right path?

Professional Triathletes Haley O'Neill and Sean Bennett are graduates from the University of Sacramento, but have no chance of landing jobs with their liberal arts degrees in the depressed economy.

Chasing the hope of winning a trip for two to Paris, the prize for each age group winner at the Freewheel Movement Triathlon in Honolulu, the young couple cashed in their frequent flyer miles, flew to Hawaii, and took their chances that one of them would win.

After losing the race, they find themselves homeless in Honolulu until a chance encounter with billionaire Bud Schubert leads them to a lifestyle beyond their wildest imaginations. Haley and Sean become the golden couple in the newly monetized sport of triathlon. They are amongst the first professional triathletes to garner prize money the likes of golf and tennis, and hire attorney Zana West to be their sports agent.

When Zana discovers that performance enhancing drugs have infiltrated the pro triathlon ranks, she enlists the help of Olympic Gold Medalist Ryan Peterson who was ousted from professional cycling for doping years ago. *VO2 Max* takes readers for a spin in the fast and newly glamorous world of professional triathlon.

Assume Guilt

A Matt Barlow Novel

Paul M. Lisnek

With loyalty, family secrets, and death involved, Matt Barlow must discover the real facts.

Attorney Matt Barlow vowed he'd never be part of a criminal case again, not after failing to save an innocent man from the death penalty. A jury consultant on civil cases, Matt doesn't waver until…

When Chicago's top real estate developer and aspiring politician Charles Marchand is charged with the death of his wife, Sandra, loyalty to an old friend pushes Matt into signing on as the jury consultant for the defense. But the case is about much more than guilt or innocence.

As Matt—and his staff—delve deeper into the evidence, they uncover information Marchand himself would just as soon stay buried, including the death of a college classmate that links him to the corrupt Leo Toland, Governor of Illinois. Before the truth and lies are untangled, Matt even finds himself secretly working with his half-brother, who just happens be on the governor's payroll.

About the Author

Charles M. DuPuy has traveled the world, seen Africa as a Peace Corps Volunteer, been a salesman and a farmer and an EMT and a magazine editor and a writer. Then he trained and worked as a physician assistant, taking him from pediatrics to geriatrics and from Maine to the Maximum Security Unit of the Santa Fe State Penitentiary. Now retired, he enjoys recreational lobster fishing in Maine, plus hunting, fishing, hiking and reading, and he loves writing. He draws on his life experiences to fill the suspenseful pages he writes, adding his own brand of humor to temper it. Charles shares a home in the Southwest with his wife, Janet, their two Westies, Jack and Nina, and their two cats, Abby and Ruby.